Eliza Daye

Poems on Various Subjects

Eliza Daye

Poems on Various Subjects

ISBN/EAN: 9783744716109

Printed in Europe, USA, Canada, Australia, Japan

Cover: Foto ©Andreas Hilbeck / pixelio.de

More available books at **www.hansebooks.com**

POEMS,

ON

VARIOUS SUBJECTS.

BY ELIZA DAYE.

' Tis not in artful measures, in the chime
' And idle tinkling of a minstrel's-lyre,
' To charm His ear, whose eye is on the heart;
' Whose frown can disappoint the proudest strains,
' Whose approbation—prosper even mine.'

COWPER.

LIVERPOOL,

PRINTED BY J. M'CREERY;

And Published for the Author, at the SUBSCRIPTION LIBRARY, *Lancaster*;
also for Mr. WALMSLEY and Mr. HOLT; for Mr. JONES, Mr. GORE,
and Messrs. WRIGHT and OAMANDY, *Liverpool*; and for Mr. JOHNSON,
St. Paul's Church Yard, *London.*

Price Seven Shillings in Boards; Hot-pressed, Seven and Six-pence.

1798.

TO THE PUBLIC.

IT is with humble diffidence I introduce my Poems to the world, confident only of
their religious and moral tendency ; I rest on that
foundation, and willingly submit their other
merits to the decision of FAIR CRITICISM.

If the work should not be found strictly
correct, I must, in justice to my printer and
myself, name my living at a distance from him ;
and the frequent and long interruptions my ill
health, and other circumstances, have occasioned
in the publication, very unfavourable to an
uniform correctness.

I hope my errata will supply any material
defects, and for the rest, I resign myself to the
candour of the public.

SUBSCRIBERS NAMES.

LONDON.

The Right Reverend the Bishop of Landaff, four copies.
The Right Honourable the Earl of Derby, three copies.

The late Mr. Bell
Mr. George Bell
Mrs. Bulkley
Mrs. Blake
Andrew Cassels, Esq.
Mr. John Ewart
Mrs. Ewart
Miss Ethrington
Miss Eddie
The Rev. James Foster
Miss Grey
Miss Gillaspy, three copies
Mr. R. Gillaspy
Mr. J. Gillaspy
The Rev. Dr. Gregory
Mrs. Gregory
Mrs. Gray
Mrs. Hill

Mrs. Starkie Heywood
—— Jervis, Esq.
The late Rev. Dr. Kippis
Miss Kelsale
Mrs. Lewin
Mrs. March
Miss Rachel Nunes
Mrs. Pailleret, two copies
Mr. Samuel Robinson
Mr. Skirrah
Mr. Sanderson
Mrs. Tattersall
Mr. Tomkins
Mrs. Walker
Mr. Walker, Lecturer in
    Philosophy, fix copies.
The Hon. Joseph Yates.

SUBSCRIBERS NAMES.

LANCASTER.

The Amicable Society
Mrs. Andrews
Mr. Armstrong, two copies
Mrs. Bell, two copies
Mr. Benson, two copies
James Barrow, Esq.
The late Jos. Berkley, Esq.
Thomas Bond, Esq.
Mrs. Brockbank
Mrs. Brayshay
Mrs. Busher
Mr. Burrow
Mr. William Blackburn
Miss Bradley
Doctor Campbell
The Rev. P. S. Charrier
Miss Dolly Capstick
Miss Maria Caton
Doctor Cassels
Mr. Charnley
Mrs. Dilworth
Mrs. Dockray
Mr. Dowbiggin
The late Mrs. Dodson
Mr. George Danson
Miss Eskrigge
Mr. Ecclestone
Mrs. France
Miss Sarah Fletcher
Mrs. Foxcroft

Miss Foster
The Rev. James Foster
Mrs. Gaskell, four copies
Mrs. Goldie, two copies
Mr. Green, three copies
C. Gibson, Esq. Quarrmore
Mrs. Gibson
The Rev. Samuel Girle
Mrs. R. Housman
Miss Hargreaves
Miss Heysham
Mr. Higgin
Mrs. Holt
Mr. Robert Hinde
Mrs. Jones
Miss Jepson
Mr. Thomas Jackson
Mrs. Lawson
The late Rev. Oliver Marton
The late Mrs. Marton
Mrs. Moore
Miss Moore
Mrs. Noble
Mr. Noble
Miss Oats
John Proctor, Esq.
Mr. Padgett, Surgeon
Mrs. T. Rawlinson, 3 copies
Miss Mary Rawlinson
Miss M. H. Rawlinson

John Rawlinson, Esq.
Miss Eliza Robinson
The late Mr. Russel
The Rev. Dr. Rigby
Mrs. Saul, High-street
Mrs. Suart
Mrs. Ben. Satterthwait
Miss Satterthwait
Mrs. Nicholas Salisbury
Miss Salisbury
Mrs. Stables

Miss Sharp
Mr. Shearson
Mrs. Threlfal
The late Mrs. Wilson
Miss Wilson
The Rev. J. Watson
The Rev. James Widdit
Miss Whalley
Mr. Wilson, Attorney
Mr. Watkinson

LIVERPOOL.

Nicholas Ashton, Esq.
Mr. A. H. Aikin
The Rev. Thomas Blundell
The Rev. William Blacow
The Rev. Thomas Bleesdale
Mr. French Bold
Mrs Brandreth
Mrs. Booth
Mrs. Brown
Miss Blundell
Miss Barnes
Mr. James Brown
Miss Bevington
Mrs. Brooks
Mrs. Beakbane
Mr. Beakbane
Mr Robert Berry
Doctor Currie
James Clegg, Esq.

Mrs. R. Couband
Mrs. Cobham
Miss Ceil
Mrs. Chubbard
Miss S. Cragg
Mr. Cross
Mr. John Conway
Miss Cheisham
Mr. Henry Clark
Mr. Copland
Mr. J. Copland
Mrs. Thos. Downward
Captain Davies
Mrs. Dickinson
Mrs. Thomas Earle
Mrs. William Earle
Mrs. Fazakerly, two copies
Mr. Ford
Mr. John Forbes, jun.

Mrs. Fairclough
Mrs. Formby
Miss Fisher
Mrs. Fallows
Mr. James Freme
Mr. Fawcett
Mr. John Foster, jun.
Mr. Farrer
Mr. J. Farrer
Mr. Gregson, two copies
Mrs. Gibson
Mr. E. Gilchrist
Mr. Thomas Grey
Mr. James Gill, two copies
Mrs. Golightly
Mrs. Grace
Mr. John Gore
Mr. Goldie
Mrs. Hardcastle
John Howard, Esq.
Mrs. Hurry
Mr. Huson
Mr. Thomas Holt, jun.
Mr. Hoskins
Mr. Hippius
Mr. William Hillary
Mr. Haslinden
Mr. Holt, Walton
Miss Huddlestone, Everton
Mr. J. Johnson
Mr. Jump
Miss King

Mr. Kearton
Mr. John Kay
The Rev. Robert Lewin
Miss Leech
Mrs. Lewtas
Mrs. Leigh, Newton
Mr. Edward Molineux
Mr. William Matthews
Mrs. Norris
Miss Nunes
Miss Newsham
Miss Newton
Mr. John Nelson
Mr. Orred
Mr. Ormandy
Mr. Thomas Oaks
The Rev. Samuel Renshaw
William Roscoe, Esq.
Mrs. Richmond
Miss Rigg
Doctor Renwick
Mr. William Renwick
Miss Smith, three copies
The Rev. Joseph Smith
Miss Spencer
Miss Seel
Mrs. Steers
Mrs. Swainson
Mrs. Smith
Mrs. Sydebotham
Miss Scott
Miss Sandback.

The Rev. Wm. Shepherd
Miss Smith, Everton
Mr. James Sill
Mrs. John Tarleton
Mr. Troutbeck
Mr. M'Vicar
Miss Underwood
Miss Mary Unsworth
Miss Esther Unsworth
Mrs. Welch
Miss Williams
Mrs. Watson
Mrs. Wilson
Mrs. Wilding
Miss Wilson
Mr. Waln
Mr. Wright
Mr. Whitehouse, jun.
Mr. W. Williams

LEICESTER.

Doctor Alexander
Mrs. Alexander

LEITH.

Mr. Brown

ALDINGHAM.

The Rev. J. Baldwin, M. D.

ANGLESEY.

William Jones, Esq.

BATH.

Doctor Parry
Mrs. Parry, two copies

BEDFORD, near LEIGH

Mrs. Thompson

BIRMINGHAM.

Mrs. Pinkerton

BOLTON.

Mrs. Ainsworth
Mr. John Noble
Miss Noble
MissM argaret Noble
Mrs. Pilkington
Mrs. Poole

CARLISLE.

Miss Bowes
The Rev. Dr. Grisdale
Miss Gilpin
Doctor Heysham
Mr. Hutchinson
Charles Nevison, Esq.
The Rev. Doctor Paley
Mrs. Pearson
Miss Kitty Pearson
Miss Pearson
Miss Waugh
Mrs. Wilkinson

CIRENCESTER.

Mr. Watkins
Mrs. Watkins

CAMBRIDGE.

The Rev. Charles Frank
The Rev. James Lambert
The Rev. John Wright

CHESTERFIELD.

The Rev. Thomas Astley, six copies
Mrs. Catharine Astley
Mrs. Harding, two copies

DERBY.

Miss Stamford
Mr. William Noble

DUMFRIES.

Mr. Kellock

EDINBURGH.

Mr. Murray
Mrs. Huntington, Hull

HORNBY.

Mrs. Parker
Mrs. Wright

KIRBY LONSDALE.

Mrs. Doran
Mrs. Gathorne

KENDAL.

Miss Gowthrop
Miss S. Gowthrop
Miss R. Gowthrop
Miss Greenhow
Mrs. Greenhow
Rev. John Harrison
Miss Holmes
Mr. Thompson
Mrs. Thompson
Miss P. Whitaker
Daniel Wilson, Esq. Dallum Tower
Mrs. Wilson

LEEDS.

Mrs. William Dunderdale

MANCHESTER.

Mrs. Alcock
The Rev. — Aubrey, Stand.
The Rev. Thomas Barnes
Mrs. Barnes
Mrs. Blackmore
Mr. Blackmore
The Rev. —— Grinderod
Mr. Samuel Hardman
Mrs. Jones, Greenhill
Mr. T. Oliphant, six copies
Miss Eliza Potter
The late Mr. James Potter
Mrs. Potter, Ardwick
Dr. Percival
Mr. Spears

MELLING.

Miss Gibson, Hipping Hall
Mr. Rimmingtou
The Rev. John Tatham
Edmund Thornton, Esq.

NEWCASTLE.

Mrs. Caldwell

NOTTINGHAM.

Mr. Joseph Lowe
Mr. Whiter

NORTHAMPTON.

Miss Milne

NEWBURY.

Mrs Bunny, three copies

PRESTON.

Rev. J. Atkinson, Walton
Ralphe Asheton, Esq.
Mrs Asheton, Cuerdon Lodge
John Butler, Esq.
Mrs. Bryer
Miss Clayton, Bamber-bridge
Mrs.G.Clayton,Lostock Hall
Mrs. Cowper, Walton
The Rev. —— Ellams
The Rev. —— Evans
The late Sir Henry Hoghton,
    Bart. three copies

Lady Hoghton, two copies
Sir Henry Philip Hoghton·
Daniel Hoghton, Esq.
Miss Hornby
Mr. Jackson, Walton
The Rev —— Middleton
Mrs. Norris
Mrs. Parker, Cuerdon, two
    copies ·
The late Mrs, Pollard, Leland
The Rev. — Rowe, Hutton
The Rev. S. Shorrocks, Ru-
    sindale
Miss Wilding

POULTON in the FIELD.

Mrs. Birkett
Mrs. William Harrison
Mr. Hull, Attorney at Law
The late Mr. Singleton
Mr. Wilson, Attorney

PORTSMOUTH.

The late General Rotheram
Miss Rotheram

PRESCOT.

John Atherton, Esq.
Mr. Hodgkinson
Mrs. Smeathman, two copies
Lieutenant Stewart
Mrs. Wareing, Knowsley,
    two copies

PLACE GREEN, KENT.

Miss Anderson

SETTLE.

Mr. George Burbeck

SELBY.

Mrs. Weddel

SEDBURGH.

The Rev. Christopher Hull

WARRINGTON.

Miss Eaton
R. Guillam, Esq Bewsey
Miss Johnson
Mrs. Knowles
Miss Sibson
Mrs. Whitwell
Miss Rebecca Watt

WHITEHAVEN.

Mr. Joseph Bell
Miss Birkett
Mr. Harriman
Miss Margaret Potter

WIGAN.

Miss Cockeran
Miss Magnall

WORKINGTON.

Miss Ellwood

WOLVERHAMPTON.

Mrs. Briscoe

YORK.

Mrs. Hunter

ISLE MAN.

Miss Christian

DUBLIN.

The Rev. George Berkeley
Doctor Bagnall
Mrs. Boe
Mrs. Crothers
Mrs. M'Donnel
George Feeling, Esq.
Miss Fanny Hincks
Mr. John Henry Haley
Mr. Alexander Humfrey
Mr. Nicholas Ford Lane
The Rev. Dr. Moody
Mrs. Malkin, two copies
Mrs. Postlethwaite
Mrs. W. Roche
Mrs. Robinson
Mrs. Sankey
Miss Taylor
Mrs. Underwood
Abraham Wilkinson, Esq.

CORK.

Miss Jane Augusta Roche

CONTENTS.

CONTENTS.

ERRATA.

Page 8, *line* 4, *read* adorn'd, for edged.
        8,   They tremble as they.
9,   7,   When winding.
        8,   Upon for on.
54,   4,   Then, for Since.
58, 11,   Mariner.
     12,   trusts and counts.
63,   8,   inspiring.
69,   2,   chains.
70,   9,   charms adorn.
71,   4,   others.
      5,   each word.
72,   3,   said.
74, 13,   humble.
76,   5,   cries.
89,   9,   Omit one of the articles.
93,   4,   is, for are.
102, 13,   powers.
103, 11,   Place the comma after like.
     13,   tree.
127, 2,   displays.
128, 23,   light, for night.
133, 21,   charms are.
135, 1,   modest doubts, for diffidence.
147, 1,   nymphs.
150, 1,   He, for She.
      8,   Only a comma, and no break in the paragraph.
153, 8,   forget.
164, 3,   all, for each.
     17,   they, for each.
168, 7,   known.
216, 10,   you, for yon.
231, 19,   design'd.
233, 13,   possest, for the best.
     16,   Must, for that.
239, 6,   shalt.
250, 11,   my contrite prayers.
255, 7,   as memory's tints are found.

POEMS.

Upon a lady losing a sprig of Myrtle, presented to her by her husband, on the morning of their marriage.

NOW beneath pale Luna's beam,
Fairies sport, while mortals dream ;
Cruel schemes they plan to-night,
Mischief charms each pigmy sprite ;
Hear, enraged, their frowning queen,
Thus exclaim, with jealous spleen ;
Shall a mortal dare be blest,
When sad Titania cannot rest?
Thwart their marriage, fairy elves,
Or scorn and hate pursue yourselves.

B

Thrice I wave my magic wand,
   Your signal to prepare ;
Obedient to your queen's command,
   Ascend the ambient air.
Five times compass round the earth
   Ere day your motions bind ;
Thence bring each scatter'd mischief forth,
   'Pandora once confin'd.
Blooms yon bower in summer's pride ?
   Soon shall my fell revenge,
Poisons in every beauty hide,
   And nature's charms shall change.
Quick as thought my elves begone,
   Impatient as my mind,
Fly swift before the tardy moon,
   And leave e'en light behind.

   Instant see the work is wrought,
See the scattered mischiefs brought ;
In Palemon's fav'rite bower,
Quick they taint each beauteous flower.
Diseases weave their baneful net,
Round the sweetest minionet.
On the jessamine's snowy breast,
Cold Indifference takes its rest ;
While Discord's evils to disclose,
It lurks within the blooming rose.

Jealousy its venom twines,
Round the greenest eglantines;
Deceit, which ever wounds unseen,
Takes the gay carnation's mien.
While beneath the woodbine's shade,
Sad Despair reclines his head,
Sullen, tainting by his power,
The freshest leaf and sweetest flower;
But the myrtle I deplore,
Of love the emblem—ah! no more.
Envy spreads her hateful sway,
All its wonted charms decay.
The hour that gives a life to joy,
Must all our anxious thoughts employ.
Palemon, early from his bower,
Plucks many a sweet and fatal flower;
And oft he would with transport cry,
I take you to a milder sky.

Accept, he said, most lov'd and fair,
The sweets which may with thee compare.
Health o'er her cheek its roses threw,
Diseases ghastly forms withdrew,
She look'd—and cold Indifference fled,
The jessamine hung its pallid head;
She spoke—the blooming rose must die,
For discord turn'd to harmony.
The eglantine was next subdued,
For jealousy can ne'er obtrude,

Where conscious worth and native sense,
Inspire a generous confidence.
Her candid speech, her heart sincere,
The gay carnation next must fear;
Honour and innocence still rise,
Superior to a low disguise.
The woodbine felt a quick decay,
For soon she smiled despair away;
Graces which other ills subdued,
Were but bitter Envy's food.
Palemon, with a cheering eye,
Observed, that beauty bloom'd to die,
But Hebe's merit still would prove,
The bond of undecaying love.
Preserving still its native hue,
Unimpair'd the myrtle grew,
Palemon vow'd to plant with care,
What withering blasts had meant to spare,
And with th' auspicious day's return,
In Hebe's breast it should be worn.
Cynthia now with silver light,
Gilds the silent hour of night;
Again the fairy tribe are seen,
And sprightly moves their alter'd queen;
She laughing tells her kinder sprite,
The mischiefs they had wrought last night.
And see, she cried, stern envy bloom,
For many a woe and wrong to come;

Swift the friend of lovers flies,
To steal the baneful cherish'd prize;
But this fair Hebe did not see,
Or would she ask an elegy?

THE

BIRTH-DAY ORNAMENTS.

PERSON and mind, we must confess,
Receive from polish and from dress
A charm to point the native grace,
The virtuous heart, the beauteous face;
But faults in each, refuse their aid,
And more adorn'd are more display'd;
Can polish'd vice the good engage ?
A viper in a gilded cage !

'Twas thus the tender parent thought,
When his adorning gifts he brought;
My child, he said, my Rosaline,
* And all the father beam'd divine,

---

* There is no affection so pure and angelic, as that of a father to a daughter. In love to our wives, there is defire; to our sons, ambition; but in that to our daughters, there is something which there are no words to express.—*Spectator*, Nº. 449.

Benignant May how cheers the earth,
And this day twelve years was thy birth;
May it be mine this day to bring,
Important treasures to thy spring.
And thy lost mother to restore,
Give thee the ornaments she wore;
For these, while here we were allied,
With love and me were all her pride.
Evander then in accents mild,
Thus with his gifts address'd his child.
My sweetest Rose, attention pay,
And fix thy thoughts on what I say;
If these from you no worth receive,
How vainly does my fondness give.
For here, the wise no value trace,
Till these are joined by kindred grace;
And first, he said, my Rosaline,
This OZIER WAND's by nature thine,
Alas! it was in Eden broke,
Evander sighing as he spoke;
The giver there how much forgot,
Ordained it your peculiar lot;
Whene'er it bends to just command,
See, how it blooms beneath the hand;
Keep it my child, with care thro' life,
It suits the daughter and the wife,
And tho' it marks no present sway,
To rising honours leads the way;

'Tis planted first in wisdom's school,
And leads the mighty to their rule.

A VEIL he next display'd to view,
Edg'd with PEARLS of blooming hue;.
He thus proceeded, these you see,
Wear the sweet blush of MODESTY;
When thus drawn forth, compell'd to shew,
Mark how trembling is the glow;
This serves you in a double sense,
An ornament and a defence;
Its timid lustre can unfold,
A sacred charm to awe the bold;
Give every beauty softer grace,
And add ideal loveliness,..
The beauteous ensign of your fame,
And woman's glory is its name;
Again he paus'd to view his child,
With timid look, she blushing smil'd.

A brilliant WATCH the next he brought,
It's chain with many an emblem wrought;
The cock, prime herald of the dawn,
The loaded bee, from flowery lawn.
Silkworms and spiders at their looms,
And ants that hoard ere winter comes;
Its worth admiring, as he viewed,.
His theme Evander thus pursued,

My Rose, 'till time shall pass away,
Be this the emblem of thy day;
With this pursue thy steady course,
'Tis action gives to virtue force,
Loitering, you as this machine,
Some spring to good have wrong within;
Winding up this splendid toy,
On yourself your thoughts employ,
And since life here, to you was given,
To fit you for a life in heaven;
Ask with every setting sun,
What for heaven has Rosaline done?

The gift that courted next her sight,
Was a clear ROBE, of SPOTLESS WHITE;
The father said, my Rosaline,
This, with its kindred grace be thine,
By all the good and wise confest,
The pride of virtue and of taste;
Free as the air, open as day,
Children this beauteous robe display.
And thence, the prince of love and peace,
Declares, of such my kingdom is;
Much merit should this gift impart,
And all its wearers shew the heart;
It is the dress which angels wear,
And thought their purest emblem here;

Evander ceased, rejoiced to see,
His child possess SIMPLICITY.

A TURBAN to adorn the HEAD,
Was the rich present next display'd ;
Gems from every country brought,
Work which every age had wrought ;
There arts and science spread their store,
In brilliant types, from every shore ;
And as its value stood confest,
Evander thus his thoughts exprest,
This gift a value must possess,
Too rich, some think, for female dress ;
Its worth to know exceeds your powers,
And nature meant it only ours ;
Whoe'er these narrow claims have spread,
But little of themselves have said ;
Little discernment have they shown,
Who have your worth so little known.
How can their rugged bosoms prove,
Exalted friendship, tender love.
By no such vanity beguil'd,
I give it thee my darling child,
Tho' in itself a boundless store,
With caution let it still be wore.
On you, it was not meant for show,
Tho' there be those who wear it so,

From all conceit, still wear it free,
Beneath the veil of modesty.
A conscious joy the father took,
From Rosaline's inquiring look,
And as his last best gift he draws,
He views it with a solemn pause,
Conceal'd the moisture of his eye,
And half suppress'd the rising sigh,
Assum'd composure ere he spoke,
And thus his tender silence broke,
Thou dearest object of my cares,
Accept the gifts my love prepares,
But vain the value of the rest,
If this, the chief, be not carest;
Then, thro' this CRYSTAL every day,
My presents carefully survey,
Thro' this, inspect my gifts of love,
How they decay, or they improve,
To what the wise shall recommend,
If fitly, meek OBEDIENCE bend,
This will a gentle firmness show,
To dignify the MODEST glow;
Display your best pursuits, and thence,
Incite to active DILIGENCE,
And by a conscience free from harm,
Show INNOCENCY's open charm,
Extending every virtue's sphere,
You see the worth of KNOWLEDGE here;

Tis thus the wise, with steady eye,
Their morals by RELIGION try,
And if with these thro' life you move,
Our joys our virtues you improve,
With fond attentions, ceaseless cares,
Tis woman guards our infant years;
Her kind compassions sooth in death,
And she receives our parting breath.

THE LAUREL.

Ah scenes belov'd in vain,
I feel the gales that from you blow.
A momentary bliss bestow,
As waving fresh their gladsome wing,
My weary soul they seem to sooth,
And redolent of joy and youth,
To breathe a second spring.

GRAY.

THAT fortune's fickle, beauty frail,
Has been the theme of many a tale,
And solemn bards, with soaring eye,
Have traced our passage to the sky.
That earthly honours quickly pass,
That life's a dream, and flesh is grass,
Are truths the preacher would impart,
In melting lessons to the heart,
And, if on beauty, wealth, or fame,
You dare to build a haughty claim,
The moralist again would try,
To wean your hearts from vanity.

Attend, ye beauties of a day,
For you I dress my moral lay,
You, who to wealth or fame aspire,
For you I tune my willing lyre.

There lived a maid, Eliza named,
Who was for nothing very famed,
With beauty she was never blest,
And this her sex can well attest,
To fortune she as little owed,
A circumstance well understood,
All her pretensions, all her aim,
Was to deserve an honest name;
With modesty to live retired,
And leave the gay to be admired,
A shepherd, skill'd in flattery's lore,
However, sent some verses to her,
He prais'd her for ideal graces,
And wrong he was in many places,
Tho' wrong, she knew he meant no evil,
And thought he was exceeding civil,
She told him, as in duty bound,
She wifh'd he were with laurel crown'd;
A nymph there was of lovely mien,
Who lived at that time on the green,
No fitter subject for his muse,
The poet sure could ever chuse;

And ready for his similies,
The earth and sky before him lies;
To him the garden yields its pride,
The mine its treasures cannot hide,
And little brooks, and mighty seas,
He pilfers with the greatest ease,
Oh! for the magic of his art,
To sooth the weakness of the heart;
And on the sunbeam of an eye,
To rise to immortality;
My humbler muse, alone must tell,
I knew the nymph and lov'd her well,
Much merit she might justly claim,
And Hannah was the fair one's name;
As cheerfully they pass'd the day,
Together oft these nymphs would stray,
And once a laurel they espy'd,
Which rais'd its head with conscious pride;
The tree a little garden graced,
And by a lowly cot was placed,
They pitied that Apollo's care,
Should waste its classic honours there,
The thought to flattering Colin led,
How much its leaves would grace his head,
Equally pleas'd with the intent,
They instant to the cottage went,
The dame, for whom the laurel grew,
No Daphne or Apollo knew,

The ladies spoke her very fair,
Told her they saw a laurel there,
If she could such a favor grant,
Some of it's leaves they soon should want ;
The dame replied, they were too good,
On such a trifle to have stood,
But near the road, and low the wall,
They might, for her, have ta'en them all ;
It was a tree she had no good in,
Except indeed to mend a pudding,
And then in winter it was green,
A time one valued such a thing,
But they were welcome to a part,
Of her tree's leaves, with all her heart.
With skilful hands, fair Hannah weaves,
Apollo's consecrated leaves,
Nor e'er before or since was seen,
So gay a garland on that green,
Its waving circles gaily play'd,
To crown the favour'd poet's head.
A sylph, who trod the rural scene,
In haste convey'd it o'er the green ;
The yielding doors soon open flew,
And full she shone on Colin's view ;
He hail'd her as a nymph divine,
She him a favourite of the Nine,
The prize of wit she then display'd,
Wishing to see it on his head.

His head—his dinner scarce begun,
On honour—less than eating run,
It is a truth the shepherd owns,
He thought of salads more than crowns:
But such a slight soon to repair,
He view'd it with attentive care,
And on its leaves he found a note,
Which simply thus the ladies wrote.

  ‘ Let gold and gems, a pond'rous weight,
‘ Surround the care-worn brow of state,
‘ And may the mournful yew be spread,
‘ O'er the cold ashes of the dead.
‘ While the gay rose and myrtle twin'd,
‘ The happy lover's temples bind.
‘ But may the head of sad despair,
‘ A wreathe of drooping willow wear.
‘ While still at friendship's sacred shrine,
‘ The vine should round the elm entwine.
‘ But when a poet we have found,
‘ With laurel shall the bard be crown'd.’

  'Twas with surprize the damsels learn'd,
The shepherd had the crown return'd.
He said Eliza ought to wear it,
Nor would he e'en pretend to share it.
Well pleas'd she kept the gilded crown,
By flattery more beauteous grown.

C

A vision now I introduce,
Is aught denied the poet's use ?
But ladies, that it need not fright,
It is no imp that shuns the light,
Or haunts the mansions of the dead,
From them it is for ever fled,
Its being rose when earth began,
And ends but with the race of man ;
Its silent path was swiftly trod,
And many victims strew'd its road,
Its hands a scythe and hourglaſs bore,
To mark its progress and its pow'r,
It touch'd the crown, which own'd its stroke,
While thus to reason's ear it spoke.—
' A boundless conqueror am I,
' Nor boast of partial victory ;
' I take this trifling toy from you,
' And mighty empires I subdue.
Her faded crown Eliza view'd,
And thus the moral thought purſued—
Faded trifle, passing jest,
Mimic pageant of a day,
No more for laurels we'll contest,
Prizes which time shall bear away.

APPEARANCE AND REALITY.

VIRTUE and *prudence* once agreed,
In Hymen's bands their lives to lead;
Their offspring daughters prov'd to be,
Appearance and Reality.
In mutual harmony they grew,
And equal joy their parents knew;
With looks serene and accent mild,
Virtue address'd her eldest child.
A parent's heart can only know,
The joys that in my bosom glow;
When I behold my first-born care,
So more than all my wishes fair.
The rose which paints thy beauteous cheek,
The snow that whitens o'er thy neck,
The gems which sparkle in thine eyes,
Fill all my soul with fond surprize,

Not only in myself I rest,
Appearance joins to make me blest,
Thy beauties every heart can warm,
And virtue thro' thy means must charm.
But oh my daughter ! hear my voice,
Thy sister's worth be still thy choice,
And boast no charm, whate'er it be,
Forgetful of *Reality*.
Her merits to the world display,
While she secures thy bounded sway.

Prudence his anxious fears confess'd,
And thus his fav'rite charge address'd,
My darling child ! in thee I find,
Thy mother's graces all combin'd,
Each feature of her lovely face,
With fond delight in thee I trace.
But let my daughter now attend,
And hear the counsels of her friend.
Tho' solid worth be all thy own,
Appearance best can make it known.
Her varied graces all admire,
Appearance every breast can fire,
Give her a place within thy heart,
And all thy worth she shall impart.

Thus hand in hand the sisters went,
And fill'd their parents with content.

Reality's more solid worth,
Appearance studied to set forth.
While she secured her sister's claim,
And gave *Appearance* spotless fame.
Their tender love soon care beguil'd,
Till virtue left her darling child,
Appearance then with forward mien,
Before her sister still was seen,
Unbounded lures around she spread,
Nor ever for her sister staid.
And such her soft attractive grace,
In every heart she found a place ;
Not long deceiv'd the wise could be,
They found she'd left *Reality*.
And soon the subjects of her reign,
Were but the thoughtless and the vain.

'Twas with contempt her sister saw,
The servile herd about her draw,
And when her father's head was laid,
She scorn'd to sue to her for aid,
But conscious of her native worth,
Without *Appearance* ventur'd forth.
Vainly she seeks to find a friend,
Her hidden merits none commend,
Without *Appearance* few would see
The merits of *Reality*.

Their error now the sisters find,
Experience shows their interest join'd,
Virtue and *Prudence* must delight,
To see their offspring still unite.

THE

FAMILY of ADVERSITY.

PART I.

The writer of this poem wishes first to confider adverfe fituations in that point of view, wherein they are productive of invention, the miftrefs of all the mechanic powers; and in the fecond place to point out how far the heart may be improved, and the underftanding enlarged, by a patient fubmiffion to thofe trials which it may be our lot to experience.

TO thee the fatal Urn* was given,
Dispenser of the wrath of heaven,
Sad treasurer of human woe!
Sparing the dire contents bestow,
Nor suddenly thy terrors pour,
O'erwhelming in th'unguarded hour.

---

* Two Urns by Jove's high throne have ever ftood,
The fource of evil one, and one of good.

Iliad, Book 24.

'Till of thy clouded gifts we learn,
Th' intrinsic value to discern :
Our joy from sorrow to procure,
And rise from ardent trials pure.

Where pleasure with her festive train,
Had shone with bright but transient reign,
By sad reverse was quickly seen,
A matron of a sordid mien.
For sofas soft—with velvet spread,
Her seats were on the broken reed;
For pearls—which golden robes adorn,
For gems—which bid the gazer turn,
Her mournful garments now display,
The veil which shades the absent day.
For melting sounds, 'twas joy to hear,
When dying on the list'ning ear,
Harsh discords still to her belong,
And hoarse the raven screams his song.
Where myrtle's fragrance did exhale,
And roses more perfum'd the gale.
The drooping willow there she view'd,
And life-destroying upas* strew'd.

---

* Where seas of glass in gay reflection smile,
  Round the green coasts of Java's happy isle ;
  Soft zephyrs blow, eternal summers reign,
  And showers prolific bless the soil—in vain !
  Fierce in dread silence on the blasted heath,
  Fell upas sits, the hydra tree of death.

BOTANIC GARDEN.

To sum the whole of earthly grace,
Where shone the mind illumin'd face,
And as the animating soul,
Gave vital vigour to the whole.
Her looks for fear alone were made,
And horror in deep furrows laid,
Where gay amusements used to cheer,
Her's were to human thought severe.
Nor costly viands suit her need,
On human tears compell'd to feed.
A fatal change her presence wrought,
And gardens into desarts brought.
The pumice stone oft mark'd her road,
And verdure faded where she trod.

Full many a child this matron bore,
And train'd them to her rugged lore,
Ruthless—her bosom could forego,
The tenderness that mothers show,
Tho' wayward tempers should misuse,
The fond caress they best can use.
By terrors only skill'd to rule,
Remorseless was her rigid school.
And yet, beneath her rugged care,
Arose a train of daughters fair,
For heaven their souls she well refin'd,
Or sent them forth to bless mankind.

'Twas soon her joy, if joy e'er came,
To train her first to deeds of fame:
Teach her aspiring eye to soar,
And give her arm unequall'd power;
And by the woes she made her feel,
Remov'd each dread of other ill.
Her massy weapons high she'd wield,
And teach how hardest rocks must yield :
They bear the print of many a wound,
And distant far her strokes resound,
Their strokes so deep, to echo tell,
Who trembling ! counts them in her cell.
And thus she said, and sternly frown'd,
Resistless I am ever found,
Heir of my fortune ! yield to fate,
I shall instruct thee to be great,
Unaw'd by threats, unchang'd by woes:
Superior still the damsel rose,
Aiming her parent to delight,
She robed herself in purest white.
All vain her fury to disarm,
For what can rugged natures charm :
And soon to urge her daughter's fate,
She led her thro' her gloomy state.
Her barren deserts first she show'd,
From these she said receive thy food.
Vainly were her intreaties made,
To guard her there her mother staid,

She turn'd her piercing eye around,
To view th' inhospitable ground.
Yet in extremity of woe,
Despair she still disdain'd to know.
At length, to meet her searching eyes,
A bended wand, well pleas'd she spies,
She seized it with presaging smile,
And oft she turn'd the barren soil;
Which as she turn'd, all fair to view,
A nymph her quick attention drew;
The golden sheaves which harvest spread,
Composed a garland for her head.
She in her hand a basket bore,
With many a plant, and seed, and flow'r,
And as a cheering look she throws,
A tree all fresh and blooming rose,
And its gay branches to entwine,
Luxuriant wound the curling vine.
This crown she said, by Ceres wrought,
To thee undaunted maid I've brought.
Vertumnus and Pomona join,
To hail thee too, with gifts divine.
Nature shall at thy touch revive,
And Flora's beauteous offspring live,
Thee I attend, aspiring maid,
To strew these gifts where thou shalt lead.
And soon a fresher verdure rose,
And soon the golden harvest glows;

Thro' fertile vallies rivers glide,
And foliage cloaths the mountain's side,
Sweet herbage decks the fragrant field,
And orchards all their treasures yield.

    Tho' in her own created ground,
No gentler was her mother found ;
Think not she said to rest thee here,
Thy glory must be purchased dear,
Then cleave for me that rugged oak,
And learn to move yon solid rock ;
Prepare thee for this wond'rous deed,
By me compell'd, thou must succeed.
Full oft she views her task severe,
With anxious thought, attentive care.
In silence bids her active mind,
Assistance for her trials find.
And many a thought repulsed again,
By many an effort weak and vain ;
Could not subdue th' aspiring aim,
To add these glories to her name ;
Till half refin'd from earthly mold,
Her mind illumin'd, could behold
The pow'r who with the gifts of gods,
Descends to comfort man's abodes.
Slow she trod the earth she bless'd,
Her silver locks a circle press'd ;

As she majestic took her way,
These words she said, or seem'd to say:
As light of day and midnight oil,
Witness'd thy unremitting toil,
To thy extended mind is giv'n
The choicest blessings under heav'n;
Reward of many an anxious hour,
Receive these gifts, and try their pow'r,
Now cleave the oak and raise the rock,
And earth's deep storehouses unlock.
The damsel saw with eager eyes,
Their wonder working power she tries.
To shew her deeds, the time would fail,
Volumes could scarcely tell the tale;
How all the treasures earth had stor'd,
She for the use of man explor'd,
And suiting to his wants applied,
And o'er the ocean was his guide;
Thro' her the weak the strong restrain,
And to their use the mighty train;
As mistress of each useful art,
She rose endear'd to ev'ry heart;
Nor here her mother seal'd her worth,
But more accomplish'd sent her forth,
And to the useful, taught to join
All that could polish and refine,
Delight the eye, enchant the ear,
And steal the spirit from its care.

Thus from a rigid parent soars,
A daughter whom the world adores,
Counting the trials she has foil'd,
All hate the mother, love the child.

THE

FAMILY of ADVERSITY.

PART II.

ADVERSITY! if e'er thy dart,
With poignant sting has touch'd my heart,
If, sick'ning to my mortal taste,
Thy cup to me has ever past;
Oh may thy wounds with soundness heal,
Thy bitter draughts with vigour fill;
That so unblamed I now may trace,
The brightest daughter of thy race;
Thy second lovely to be seen,
Of tend'rest heart and mildest mein,
With each engaging grace her own,
Ne'er charm'd away her mother's frown.
Who ever, strange as it appears,
Seem'd most delighted with her tears;

Yet skill'd to torture, joy she show'd,
And mock'd her with delusive good.

Of me severe, the offspring mild,
Hear me, she said, obedient child;
All fair to view, from me receive,
The portion I deceitful give;
Smiling malignant as she rose,
There if thou can'st, she said, repose.
Then on with sullen step she leads,
The path her child obedient treads;
Possess, she said, by my command,
Fit scenes for a correcting hand,
Whose prospect now delights thine eyes,
The fairy land of promises;
Where my gay sister keeps her court,
Where all the willing world resort,
To taste the bounties of her store,
Which few enjoy but all adore.
Her dangerous gifts let VIRTUE fear,
And still remember I am near.

New charms still nearer views display'd,
As onward goes the artless maid;
Each flatt'ring scene subdued its part,
And shared the feelings of her heart,
And now the form appear'd in view,
Whose charms surrounding vot'ries drew.

With brilliance dress'd, with fragrance crown'd,
And hands that spread her favours round.
As from an urn, all to delight,
She drew her treasures infinite.
Whate'er employ'd a mortal care,
All that inspir'd a hope was there.
Health's vital vigour nerv'd the strong,
Pleasure's soft charms allur'd the young,
She honour's purple robe bequeaths,
And blind ambition's random wreathes;
Grandeur to vacant pride affords,
And fills the grasping miser's hoards:
She pomgranates and myrtles joins,
And loves perennial bands entwines;
Beauty was there—the world to charm,
And wit—that could the wise disarm:
And gratitude, and perfum'd praise,
That gifts enhance, and merits raise.
She flatt'ry's honey'd poison draws,
To swell the vain, with false applause,
She friendship's purest flame could light,
And there the vine and elm unite.

The urn, the nymph with transport views,
And meekly to the goddess sues:
Pity she said my state forlorn,
To hatred of my parent born;

D

Me rescue from a doom so hard,
And from that parent be my guard.
A languid look the goddess gave,
Again she pleads her pow'r to save,
While prostrate she that pow'r ador'd,
She humbly thus her gifts implor'd.

I pour not here my humble pray'r,
For joy which takes no tint of care;
   For more myfelf to know,
Goddess, perhaps thy gifts bestow'd,
To me were the securer good,
   Chasten'd by shades of woe.

Yet smooth my rugged parent's frown,
Her thorns, oh may thy roses crown;
   Thy light, her shades among,
With vernal hope rise ever new,
While timid fear of changing hue,
   Warns my approach to wrong.

Bestow thine aromatic wreathe,
While here the vital air I breathe,
   With health my temples bind,
If there should mix some faded leaves,
For transient pain my bosom grieves,
   Shall joy be more refin'd.

Now meek contentment's olives bring,
Let cheerfulness her rubies fling,
   Upon my sighing breast.
With syren song, and transient rose,
By giddy youth be pleasure chose,
   Repented when possest.

May blind ambition's random crown,
Be on disorder'd passion thrown,
   Which aims some airy height,
But honour's purple robe bestow,
Whose guiltless smile, and open brow,
   Shall more than fame delight.

Of gold I ask no mighty store,
I shrink from fortune's dangerous pow'r,
   Yet oh, that share impart;
Which leaves a little to bestow,
To ease some want of sighing woe,
   Raise, not corrupt my heart.

The passion and the tender care,
While wealth and beauty amply share,
   Be mine the safer helm;
Of friendship at whose hallowed shrine,
Oh goddess! now for me entwine
   The vine around the elm.

Sincerity, of heart so pure,
With confidence that rests secure,
  And faith's unbroken seal ;
Solicitude so swift to serve,
With constancy that cannot swerve,
  Her presence shall reveal.

Her pray'r to hear the goddess seems,
And smiles her into golden dreams,
And health's fresh rose and balmy wreathes,
The goddess freely now bequeathes.
But soon her mother touch'd the crown,
All its salubrious sweets are flown :
Hemlock and deadly nightshade now,
Compose a garland for her brow ;
And ev'ry boon the goddess gives,
Her mother blasts as she receives.
And now she frown'd upon her view,
Nor more the nymph could joy pursue.
No more, she said, my sister seek,
In gifts revers'd 'tis I who speak,
Now tainting health's salubrious gale,
I bring disease, and thou art pale ;
But ask thy heart, and it shall tell,
What blessings may with sickness dwell ;
It early calms all anxious strife,
For the frail vanities of life ;

The brittle tenure of thy days,
It marks, and wisdom guides thy ways;
Another's pain to thee reveals,
And all thy soften'd bosom feels.
I wave with scorn the peacock's plumes,
And honour's purple robe consumes,
From slander's tongue, and pride's parade,
Receive a grace which cannot fade;
Slander and scorn themselves deceive,
Then nobly pity and forgive;
Thine innocence thy breast shall calm,
And crown thee with thy native palm;
I by injustice turn the scales,
And thy expected treasure fails;
But inward turn and there explore,
Resources unperceiv'd before,
What prosp'rous days awhile conceal'd,
Adverfity has oft reveal'd;
As stars, obscured by dazzling light,
Adorn the sable brow of night;
For gratitude so rich in store
To make the benefactors poor;
I overpow'ring ivy bring,
And the embosom'd adder's sting.
If what thy bounty could impart
Flow'd from the feelings of thy heart,
The joys thy kind intentions earn,
Arise above a base return;

For praise which merit might enhance,
I bring thee envy's bas'lisk glance;
And for the concord of the heart,
Point enmity's keen forked dart;
The dying fern and choaking reed,
To love's perennial bands succeed.
The vine shall bind the elm no more,
Nor friend protect, nor love adore.
These bitter dregs, now drain my bowl,
And purify thy spotless soul.

Of me severe, the offspring mild,
I give the world my darling child.
Above all theory of speech,
To live the lessons others teach;
Her presence solitude shall cheer,
And ev'ry public bliss endear;
With equal fortitude shall own,
A martyr's, or a monarch's crown.

Tho' many were the numbers more,
Of children whom this matron bore,
Than these among the shining race,
None more exalted could we trace;
Their hearts to soften, minds enlarge,
Was her severe and fav'rite charge.

CHLOE.

PAINTER exert thy utmost art,
To shew the fav'rite of my heart;
Roses and lilies thou may'st spare, .
Chloe can please, yet is not fair;
Thy Venus may the world admire,
It is to Chloe I aspire;
One added grace should'st thou display,
My Chloe's charms would fade away;
Let nature on thy canvass shine;
It is my Chloe! 'tis divine!

Be Chloe's mind the poet's theme,
No fancied merits let him dream;
O'er fair perfection should he rove,
It is a mortal that I love;
Yet goodness in my Nymph I see,
Or Chloe had no charms for me:
Let truth and nature teach his tongue,
And artless Chloe grace his song.

He sings her generous and sincere,
And there my Chloe must appear.
A sister's merits she'll commend ;
My Chloe too, can be a friend,
All gay and lively tho' she be,
Can melt in tenderest sympathy.
See truth and nature grace each line,
It is my Chloe ! 'tis divine !

TO ———

THO' faintly shines this winter's sun,
   And short his visits be,
He warms my heart, for oft I hope,
   He shines on you and me.

The moon too, beauteous queen of night,
   Enraptur'd still I see;
For sure I think her rays serene,
   Are seen by you and me.

And gaily burns our rural fire,
   And happy should I be,
But cold's my heart, there wants a charm,
   It warms not you and me.

And fiercely blows this cold north wind,
   For ruffian blasts has he ;
But bitterer far that zephyr's breeze,
   Which parted you and me.

TO ANNA.

Basking thus in fortune's way,
Would you leave so bright a day?
See the captive lover wait,
Must you die to seal his fate?
Hark! the poet tunes his lyre,
Cruel! would you damp his fire?
Balmy zephyrs court your breath,
Not the bitter blasts of death:
Bright in youth and beauty's charms,
Do you seek his icy arms?
Oh must friendship plead in vain,
Can you give so keen a pain?

Once, as ancient stories tell,
Music prov'd its pow'r in hell;
Music in the hand of love,
E'en the ear of death could move,

And its adamantine chains
Melted at harmonious strains.
Live, and bloom in fortune's ray,
While she gives so bright a day.
Live, and be the poet's theme,
Feed the rapture of his dream ;
Let a friendship most refin'd,
Beam its comforts on your mind ;
Softer than a western breeze,
It shall breathe to give you ease,
All affection can inspire,
Apollo's wit and Orpheus' lyre.

SONG.

———————

SINCE Colin appear'd on our plains,
  Our village is happy and gay;
His presence enlivens the year,
  And winter is pleasing as May.

Tho' he lives the delight of the fair,
  No envy their bosoms alarms;
His good-nature so flatters them all,
  Each maid thinks him won by her charms.

But I, tho' so friendless and poor,
  He says am the choice of his heart;
And sure I shall trust in a swain,
  Who never descended to art.

I speak of the belles of the town,
  I tell him how handsome they be;
But merit the shepherd admires,
  And he fancies he finds it in me.

How much then to Colin I owe,
  Each action of life shall impart;
While it speaks in the glance of my eye,
  It shall live in the wish of my heart.

I'll rise with the break of the dawn,
  And neat shall our cottage be seen,
In Summer, how fragrant and gay,
  In Winter, so warm and so clean.

TO BELINDA.

THE wing'd inhabitant of air,
  Thro' nature freely roves,
And his harmonious notes proclaim,
  'Tis liberty he loves.

Till doom'd by some relentless hand,
  To share a pris'ner's fate,
He flutters round his narrow cell,
  And pecks his iron grate.

Vainly he tries his plaintive notes,
   And struggles to be free;
Till wearied nature bids him yield ·
   To sad necessity.

Soon in his little cage he finds
   What nature gave before,
And banish'd from his safe retreat,
   'Twere liberty no more.

When thus Belinda you had fixed
   Gay Strephon in your chains,
You doubtless thought your captive swain,
   A conquest worth your pains.

Free as the feather'd songster once,
   He tells you with a sigh,
That life and freedom's in your chains,
   But death in liberty.

EXTEMPORE LINES,

To a Young Lady with an Anemone.

———————

IN loves soft empire, beauty boasts to reign;
Yet beauty's queen once mourn'd her empire vain,
Unmoved by scorn, her undiminish'd truth,
Changed into this gay flower the breathless youth,
The worth of constant woman still to raise,
So tell the fabled tales of ancient days.

The fair Narcissus oft your favour tried,
And oft you threw the scented fop aside ;
Here native beauty, vivid colours glow,
Your present vot'ry is no perfum'd beau ;
His honour'd station be a lady's breast,
His charter held, from what he once possess'd.

TO AMANDA,

On her recovery from sickness.

WHEN April turns his wat'ry eye,
   That stain'd his infant cheek with tears,
And beneath a golden sky,
   The blooming May appears ;
Waked by the tears which April shed,
Gay Flora leaves her sleeping bed,
   And calls her beauteous train,
To hail a scene, so sweet, so fair,
Each artless warbler fills the air
   With an enchanting strain.

Sad Philomela's mournful songs,
   Chaste Cynthia's silver beams invite,
Melodiously to speak her wrongs,
   To the pale shades of night.

While the shrill lark salutes the morn,
And hails the God of Day's return,
   With many a sprightly lay;
Gay flowers present their fragrant bloom,
Mild zephyrs catch the rich perfume,
   To scent the op'ning day.

Not the sweet warblers of the grove,
   Nor the shrill lark's exalted strain;
Hail more pleased the scenes they love,
   More welcome Flora's train,
Than I, when health her roses shed,
Upon Amanda's drooping head,
   And rais'd her languid frame;
Would bid my Muse, her transports show,
And paint the sympathetic glow,
   Inspired by friendship's name.

Not flowers more freely spread their bloom,
   More freely their rich fragrance bring,
The gentle zephyr to perfume,
   And deck the lap of Spring,
Than would I now cull ev'ry sweet,
Hygeia's lovely form to greet,
   And bless that healing pow'r,
Who opens on Amanda's sight,

E

Rejoicing friends,. renew'd delight,
　Led by each golden hour.

Far gayer garlands I had wove,
　But sullen grief, and anxious care ;
Stole them from the hand of love,
　And placed a cypress there*.
Sportive, as fancy's frolic dream,
Euphrosyne had graced my theme,
　My cheerful lyre had strung ;
But grief and fear oppos'd her reign,
And Philomela's pensive strain,
　Must hang upon my tongue.

---

* The death of one friend, and dangerous illness of another.

ON THE

DEATH of a FRIEND.

———————

AH me! then is Philida gone?
    But now! and so blythe as they tell?
Yes, hark! her mild spirit is flown,
    I hear my poor Philida's bell.

Stern death counts the Virtues his foes,
    For they parry a while his fierce dart;
So he learnt where they met to repose,
    And struck gentle Philida's heart.

I'll wander by moon-shine along,
    I'll seek out some shadow retir'd,
For Philida lov'd not a throng,
    Nor bustle or grandeur admir'd.

And near it I'll pensively stray,
 I'll watch 'till its soft tints shall fade;
For pity I'll beg it to stay,
 And think it is Philida's shade.

The west breeze I hear softly blow,
 And my harp's sweetest chords it employs;
The sounds tho' they mournfully flow,
 Sooth not like my Philida's voice,

She is gone! in friendship and love,
 Here no more shall I Philida see;
A span, and I too shall remove,
 And happy near Philida be.

TO THE MEMORY OF

THE LATE RÉV. C—— R——.

WHERE heavenly precept bright example taught,
And truths divine, a clear conviction wrought;
Aided by that persuasive eloquence,
The charm of language, and the force of sense.
When death has silenc'd that instructive speech,
Nor more that tongue important truths shall teach;
While memory's darling records she can trace,
In characters no time or change erase.
The muse her mournful tribute humbly pays,
For ever true to friends of former days:
Returning health seem'd lighting up his eye,
And rais'd his drooping friends to transient joy;
When, in behalf of injur'd Afric's claim,
To fair humanity he gave his name.
' If this, the latest act from me requir'd,
' The last is good,' he said, and—he expir'd.
So set the Christian, so his glories rise,
As summers suns descend in azure skies.

THE THREE LAMPS;

OR,

THE HERMIT OF THE WOOD.

————

OBEDIENT to th' omnipotent command,
Nature confess'd its mighty former's hand;
First smiling vegetation gaily rose,
Since, o'er the earth, unconscious beauty glows;
And from that heavenly spark that spread his sway,
Was kindled animation's vital ray.
By fine degrees extending still the plan,
To godlike reason, and imperial man,
Highly endow'd, the sov'reign of the whole,
Nor him the swift escape, nor strong control.
O'er earth he sits on an unquestion'd throne,
A tributary here to God alone;
Nor are his views alone to earth confin'd,
To higher views are needful aids assign'd.

Meanly content or arrogantly bold,
Then let not man his faith and hope withhold.
Let faith and hope imperfect virtue aid,
And finite—own what infinite has said.
Come dress me fiction for the ear of youth,
Some tale that shall impress the sacred truth.

In days remote, and in a distant clime,
The place and date unchronicled by time ;
Alcestes lived, the wonder of his age,
His country loved and prided in the sage ;
All bounteous heaven enrich'd his copious store,
With kind affections, and persuasion's pow'r ;
If earth too strongly once had drawn his mind,
One early trial earth-born cares refin'd ;
Sudden he lost, in pride of blooming years,
The lovely partner of his joys and cares:
His patient tears were sown with future praise,
And quench'd the sanguine hopes of following days;
He mark'd the good and ill as equal given,
A guide thro' time and death, to life and heaven ;
And on a mind so temper'd, heaven bestow'd,
Its needful aids to keep his heavenly road ;
Then who so fit the traveller to convey,
And guide the inexperienc'd in their way.

Philario's sons his anxious cares divide,
For them were fortune, cares, and pray'rs employ'd.

Love still more 'fearful, as it more endears,
Gave him the anxious joys of hopes and fears;
He oft their virtues and their faults would try,
And scan them with a parent's watchful eye;
As heirs of heav'n, his sons he fondly view'd,
Nor his low aim confin'd to earthly good;
Early exalting his unclouded powers,
His oldest son to learning gave his hours;
By philosophic virtue firmly arm'd,
By moral beauty was Eugenio charm'd;
Unaided by high hopes or coward fear,
All for itself to him was virtue dear;
.Worthy the scale he held in nature's plan,
Approv'd by reason, and becoming man.
As toys or bugbears, children please or fright,
Rewards and punishments were motives light,
Hence in Philario's breast foreboding fears,
Hence self-dependent virtue, drew his tears.

The loves and graces smil'd on Philo's morn,
And all the charities his soul adorn;
From generous feelings, Philo's actions move,
And all his God was form'd of peace and love;
He joy'd to hope rewards for virtue given,
But thought no stern decree could flow from heaven;
His gentle nature, stranger to offence,
Treated the vicious with benevolence;

He said for misery God no being gave,
And e'en the guilty, mercy meant to save;
With joy his father view'd his virtues mild,
Yet would he mourn one error of his child,
That thro' his actions tho' they sweetly shone,
Those virtues sat on an unguarded throne.

The fair perfections which his brother own'd,
With admiration soon Ascanius found;
Candid, his less attainments soon could see,
But those he guarded by humility;
His knowledge would by patient labour earn,
Nor ever deem'd himself too wise to learn;
The dread of pain and prospect of reward,
His heart accepted, as its firmest guard.

Such were the sons who won each tender part,
Each anxious feeling of Philario's heart,
His happiest hours were with their virtues shar'd,
Nor tender lessons to their faults he spar'd;
But habits ever strengthen in their course,
And lessons oft repeated lose their force;
That truth might be with novelty convey'd,
The careful father sought for foreign aid;
His searches met the sages high renown,
For wisdom and for virtue fully known;
To him Philario sought his doubts to paint,
And pour'd his soul in many a fond complaint;

Pity he said, and hear me reverend sage,
So heaven support thee in declining age ;
Thy counsels to my need then straight display,
And aid me, far as human wisdom may ;
Thy deeds are wisdom, and thy trust is God,
Then who so fit to mark a dubious road ;
Three virtuous sons I have, my age's pride,
To fame on earth, and to heaven's hopes allied ;
Oh ! may their virtues ne'er their hearts forsake,
Nor those high hopes be lost by sad mistake,
As fares the mariners who near the shore,
Trust the false calm and count the dangers o'er,
When sad reverse, he thoughtless meets between,
The sudden tempest, and the rock unseen,
All unprovided with the means to save,
For home and safety he must meet a grave.
The means are heaven's, Alcestes gently said,
By my success be confidence repaid ;
To morrow, e'er the orb serene of night,
Gives her chaste beam for Sol's departed light ;
Let me receive thy treasures to my care,
The closing day I ever end with prayer ;
As to high heaven events are only known,
So sanctified be mortal works begun.

Philario leaves the sage with thanks exprest,
And lighten'd were the cares that weigh'd his breast;

The sage's message to his sons he broke,
And highly of his worth and wisdom spoke.
The youths with fond attention catch the strain,
And chide the hours that yet their steps detain.
Eugenio's fancy, in Alcestes finds,
Those equal pow'rs that charm in kindred minds,
Thinks how the depths of science they'll explore,
And to exalted heights of knowledge soar;
Or how they shall define th' unerring plan,
Which honour draws for rectitude in man.
Fix virtue in her independent sphere,
Unaided by reward or abject fear ;
With warm impatience Philo's bosom glows,
To such a friend his feelings to disclose ;
Revolves the joy that sympathy imparts,
When generous feelings bind congenial hearts ;
And while such sympathies their hearts expand,
They shall not, marking mercy's sparing hand,
Deem punishment annex'd to man's offence,
But clasp the scheme of wide benevolence.

Ascanius hopes to hear by him defin'd,
Heaven's mercy with its justice how combin'd ;
Those high rewards that meet the happy saint,
The joys of heaven, he longs to hear him paint ;
Potent, the strong temptation to defeat,
Speak the dire scenes th' impenitent await ;

Each thinks Alcestes as himself believes,
And thus the intermediate time deceives.

'Twas when the virgin yields her brilliant sway,
And temper'd seasons smile in equal day,
Philario's sons, by youthful ardor bent,
To greet Alcestes' mansion joyful went.
In youth's gay season, when few cares annoy,
Alive to present and to future joy,
Imagination aids each scene to warm,
And paints each beauty with a heighten'd charm;
More gay to them, reviving spring is seen,
More fresh, the verdure of its tender green;
More richly wafts the fragrance of the air,
Unclouded dawns the promise of their year,
More sweet, the season crown'd with Flora's rose,
Where ripen'd beauty summer's suns disclose;
Where splendor, fragrance, and soft harmony,
Meet health's full sense and fancy's vivid eye;
So, to the youths now more majestic shone,
Illustrious autumn, on her golden throne,
Queen of the year, they see her now display,
The gifts which tributary seasons pay;
The blushing orchard, and the waving corn,
Beneath her painted skies her reign adorn;
Nor lost to them, her colours now expand,
As her rich tints display her changing hand.

Thus pleas'd they leave their parent and their home,
And now most pleas'd they see Alcestes' dome.
Midway, adown a mountain's woody side,
The mansion rose in venerable pride;
Midst rocks and groves it rose in stately show,
And seem'd the sovereign of the vale below;
Where the gay scenes that struck the wond'ring eye,
Seem'd empires of each rural deity;
Her golden banners Ceres there display'd,
And Flora's lovely children paint the mead;
Pomona o'er the hedgerow spreads her blush,
And with rich purple decks the lowly bush;
Amidst tall firs, and solemn-seeming yew,
The village church, there steals upon the view;
As just emerging from surrounding shade,
It gives a decent order to the glade.
Hills rise on hills, to lead th' extended eye,
Till with its kindred blue, they mix in sky.
Its streams collecting, gathering still new force,
Between, a river takes its rapid course;
A careful debtor, and a subject free,
Hast'ning its willing waters to the sea.
From scenes like these their soften'd hearts imbibe,
What most have felt, but few can well describe.

Alcestes now advances to their view,
Whom the appointed time to meet them drew;

Serene as eve, as autumn rich to bless,
He seem'd the genius of his native place;
With hasten'd step, Philario's sons he meets,
And thus in accents mild their coming greets,
Welcome young friends, your presence pleases more,
As thus observant of an old man's hour,
For faith and truth Philario's sons be known,
Tho' youth to folly and neglect is prone,
Our course of friendship shall be safely trod,
Hope marks the end, when we begin with God;
From dignity serene, and mild benevolence,
These words mix awe with gentle confidence.
He leads them thro' the winding of the wood,
To where the chapel of the mansion stood,
In decent order all the household there,
Attend the blessing of their master's pray'r,
And there th' observance of the world they shun,
Thus ev'ry day was closed, and morn begun;
No warm disputes, or lectures oft as vain,
Employ the hours of eve that yet remain,
But thro' the harmless jest, or story's course,
Instruction lost its name, but took its force.

Philario's sons with admiration fraught,
An humbler notion of themselves are taught,
Their recollected vanity regret,
And view their wisdom as a counterfeit;

Their hearts, late nature's lovely scenes expand,
And now they own a master's skilful hand ;
Freeing from blind opinion to receive,
Th' important lesson which he wish'd to give;
Dressing his purpose in a pleasing view,
Which they as entertainment only knew;
Long as delightless, linger joyless years,
Swift fly th' aspiring moments friendship shares;
As high in wisdom and refin'd in taste,
All seem'd a wonder that the sage possest ;
Nor aught escaped them as they took their way,
Passing along to where their chambers lay.
And now, as still prepared for new delight,
A gallery stored with pictures struck their sight,
There many a sage and patriot appear'd,
Who blest in life, and were in death rever'd,
Not those whose dubious worth high fortune crown'd,
But whom unquestion'd merit had renown'd ;
Amongst the many which they wond'ring saw,
Three more than all their fix'd attention draw;
The painter's zeal his magic hand obey'd,
And almost life and breath his forms display'd,
One narrow path to a bright mansion led,
Along the landscape, o'er the canvass spread ;
Three figures pass it with a different fate,
And draw our admiration and regret,
While one with steady eye surveys the ground,
Keeps firm the path, and is with honour crown'd,

The others leave it, and with wand'ring feet,
Tho' they approach to bliss, destruction meet;
These pictures long their curious eyes detain,
And much they wish their meaning to explain,
Why the same landscape o'er the three are spread,
And whence the different figures there display'd;
At early matins they with joy attend,
And anxious wait the coming of their friend,
Hearts open to his counsels they prepare,
And join him in devotion's ardent prayer;
The cow bestows them her salubrious treat,
And bread and fruits their wholesome meal compleat,
Enraptur'd of the pictures now they speak,
And for their meaning to Alcestes seek;
Oh deign, they said, the mystery to relate,
And why those figures meet such different fate;
Then to the gallery straight their host they lead,
And point the pieces which they wish to read;
Alcestes view'd them with a wishful eye,
And ere he spoke, he heav'd a feeling sigh;
'Tis there, he said, enraptured with the theme,
The painter gives to sight the poet's dream,
For him entwines a never fading wreath,
And almost bids his airy phantoms breathe;
Nor to the painter give we all the praise,
But now attend to what the legend says;
This said, a scroll of parchment next he shews,
And thus proceeds its legend to disclose;

LEGEND.

The longest day in night must die,
  And winter ends the year :
And so to contemplation's eye,
  Must human life appear.

Herman had fourſcore winters past,
  His latest thread was ſpun :
Of many days he liv'd his last,
  And view'd life's setting sun.

Yet ere his spirit took its leave
  Of all it valued here ;
One fond embrace he fain would give,
  And bless his children dear.

His children dear approach his couch ;
  My sons he faintly said,
My heart still rests where I've lov'd much,
  And shrinks from death with dread.

The parting stroke, were death no strife,
  'Tis agony to bear ;
From those who gave it's joy to life,
  And ev'ry pleasing care.

Yet, ere my latest sand is shed,
  And while a breath I draw,
F

May filial duty, from this bed,
   Retain a father's law.

No well fill'd coffers you'll receive,
   Or aught of wealth or cost,
But ah ! a mansion I would give,
   Which distant realms can boast.

And sure it was my anxious care,
   To fit you for the road ;
And while I warn'd the danger there,
   The high reward I shew'd.

As thro' the wilderness no more
   A pilot to your youth,
Be dying words, my living pow'r,
   And your support, your truth.

And now they clasp his clammy hands,
   Bathe them with many a tear,
And vow, his ever lov'd commands
   Are more than life's blood dear.

'Tis well he said, the pow'r is good,
   Who grants me strength to say,
The holy hermit of the wood,
   Shall best direct your way.

Thus Herman breath'd his last adieu,
  Low in the dust he lies;
And pious prayers and honours due,
  Before his ashes rise.

His children dear, with honours meet,
  Have mourn'd the pious dead;
And next the sainted sage they greet,
  Who bless'd the solemn shade.

Hail holy hermit! oft they cry,
  Thy suppliants are we,
And meek they raise th' imploring eye,
  And low they bend the knee.

Oh! mark us out the safest way
  To a bright mansion given;
For well thou canst, that saint did say,
  Whose spirit rests in heaven.

With pious hands his mortal part,
  Beneath the green sward laid,
And with the mourning of the heart,
  His funeral honours paid.

His dying and his strict command,
  'Tis thus we have pursu'd;

When we implore thy guiding hand,
　Oh hermit of the wood !

The hermit rais'd them from the ground,
　And cheering was his look ;
Compassion in his face they found,
　And in the words he spoke.

For well of all the hermit knew,
　In past nor future scant,
To holy men, 'twas held as true,
　Heaven did such knowledge grant.

Far as my faithful word may guide,
　The holy hermit said,
My counsel shall not be denied,
　To those who seek my aid.

He took them to his simple cell,
　Of fare he gave his best :
Bright water from the purest well,
　And fruits of dainty taste.

And then around each neck he threw,
　A chain of purest gold;
Which, to each breast a lock so true,
　In forms of anchors hold.

Tho' small in size, of countless worth,
  Three lamps the chain suspend,
And thus the hermit well set forth,
  Their value and their end.

Sons of my friend! I hold you dear,
  Accept these gifts of love:
These answers to your prayers appear,
  And your true guides shall prove.

And now he takes them to the grove,
  And shews the prospect round :
And points out with parental love,
  Where the safe path is found.

Beyond he says your country lies,
  Nor rest in aught beneath ;
That narrow path commands the prize,
  Which Herman did bequeath.

Tho' narrow, and too little trod,
  These lamps shall guide your feet,
Be your conductors thro' the road,
  And find yon blest retreat.

They were not wrought by mortal hand,
  Observe and mark them well,

These lights two different views command,
  To lead and to repel. .

By each your way be ever known,
  Tho' some might seem more fair.
Thro' this is the bright region shewn,
  That crowns your course of care.

The last from specious snares shall warn,
  Still potent to disclose ;
Altho' some transient charm adorns,
  The depth of hidden woes.

I mark impatience in each eye,
  Thus youth is wont to be ;
Still ardent unknown scenes to try,
  Ere they their dangers see. .

Yet for a moment I detain,
  And further counsel hold ;
Whate'er I gave and said were vain,
  If aught remain'd untold.

While mindful of their destin'd use,
  Their owners these employ ;
As them no mortal could produce,
  No mortal can destroy.

But with such sacred art combin'd,
  And so united glows,
That one neglected still you'll find,
  Shades o'er the other throws.

Well, Herman's sons observe my words,
  So speed you in your course,
And may the counsel you've implor'd,
  Be your secure resource.

And much he grieved their thoughtless haste,
  Which scant their thanks could spare ;
And fear'd those counsels must be waste,
  Which scarce to hear they bear.

Till sight could them no more disclose,
  The Hermit's eyes pursued ;
Then care to sooth, with calm repose,
  He sought his native wood.

Together yet their pilgrim feet,
  The bidden path pursue ;
Observe the bonds for kindred meet,
  And to their faith keep true.

And bitterly I trust was rued,
  That pride which first begun,

Pernicious counsels to intrude,
  In Herman's oldest son.

This present from our friend, he says,
  Was made with kind design;
But as I cannot need its aid,
  I think but light of mine.

To some it were a potent spell;
  The weak are prone to err,
And ignorance, I know it well,
  Is moved by hope and fear.

Then this he said, and touch'd the spring,
  To others may have use,
To me, a poor and trifling thing,
  My path, I know and chuse.

And potent were those words to lose,
  The talisman that bound,
The sacred charm around his neck,
  That shew'd his safest ground.

Ah! charm no more, the anchor fails,
  The links desert the chain;
The lamp a lasting darkness veils,
  Nor fear or hope remain.

In conscious virtue all elate,
  His wisdom was his pride,
He parts, as from a vain conceit,
  With an unerring guide.

He yet a while the path pursues,
  Tho' some appear more fair;
Some dangers too, he well subdues,
  Which he encounters there.

Such snares and dangers yet he tried,
  As haughty minds can scorn,
But those which are to pride allied,
  It ever ill has born.

As o'er the youth his gentle nature yearns,
To the first painting then Alcestes turns;
Observe he said, in Herman's oldest hope,
High thoughts of self, which ill to counsel stoop,
He views the country with familiar air,
As if he deem'd a guide superfluous there:
Yet there is something noble in his mein,
The traits of honour, and a soul within;
But much I fear the legend will disclose,
That airy honour meets with potent foes:
Foes, which his lamp had sov'reign power to check,
But that you see is falling from his neck;

Sovereign by shewing to the traveller's eye,
The high reward of glorious victory;
Shewing the scenes that fallen virtue wait,
A sovereign warning from its dreadful fate:
Dark is the guide and dubious is the way,
Its end, you see no glorious prize display;
Its dangerous wanderings, there inspire no dread,
No gulphs of fire are seen, or horrors spread;
But now the legend will those scenes relate,
Which self-exalted virtue mourns too late:

For now, adapted to his mind,
    See lofty hills invite;
He leaves the humbe vale behind,
    To climb the envied height.

Vainly affection prompts his stay,
    With brethren once so dear;
Vainly they point the safer way,
    The bliss or danger near.

The apt temptation, strong of power,
    A weak defence o'erthrows;
As broken bulwarks guard the shore,
    When mighty seas oppose.

And now the giddy height he gain'd,
    Nor thought of gulphs below:

But ill the slippery path sustain'd,
  Along the mountain's brow.

Alass, he dreamt of solid bliss,
  And straight was seen no more :
'Twas fear'd he found a dread abyss.
  A deep without a shore.

Now to the painting, see him gain'd the height,
And how his looks express his vast delight :
No air more suited, could ambition breathe,
But quite conceal'd the gulph which yawns beneath :
The gulph which finishes his mad career,
And on its brink you see him next appear ;
One foot upon the sloping surface see,
The next, within the dread abyss must be :
To save a mortal tongue the dreadful tale,
See charity prepared to spread her veil ;
The motto there in golden letters read,
Judge not of him, but shun the sinner's meed.

The second painting now we should explain,
And to the legend must return again :

His rashness, oft his brothers mourn,
  And much they doubt his fate ;
How sad 'tis needful aid to scorn,
  They fear he found too late.

Another's errors ever meet
  Our wonder and our blame;
Nor think what may our peace defeat,
  And blast our virtuous name.

'Twas ill the second brother said,
  The hermit's gift to slight;
To me he added, 'tis a prize,
  View'd by the pleasing light.

The other was to me no store,
  So perish'd by neglect;
To use it was to keep its pow'r,
  So did the sage direct.

Ill-fated youth! so said the sage,
  And further said most true;
One clouded, did he well presage,
  Would shade the other view.

Distant and faint those prospects rise,
  Which glory would disclose;
And darkness only meets the eyes,
  Where terrors should oppose.

But yet, a while he safely treads,
  Charm'd by a distant good;

Nor yet ambition's glare misleads,
  Dangers or toils subdued.

But ah! yon flattering scene beware,
  Yon way so like the true;
That pleasure's near enticing snare.
  Cheat not the distant view.

Whether that road may guide as near,
  He said I soon shall learn;
If wrong, when there it shall appear,.
  'Tis easy to return.

Misguided youth! thy hopes are vain,
  Thy rash resolve I grieve;
For never more shalt thou regain,
  What thoughtless thou shalt leave.

All vain a brother's tears may flow,
  He thinks it causeless grief;
His lamp reveal'd him nought of woe,
  Nor counsel gain'd belief.

Dread pits, which sedgy verdure o'er
  Had speciously conceal'd;
As now the traveller's feet explore,
  Are fatally reveal'd.

Careless of warning, perish'd he,
  Who came so near the prize;
Then whilst we pity, let us be
  By sad example wise.

And now my youthful friends, Alcestes cries,
To the next painting I would lead your eyes;
The dullest eye may note the temper here,
Benevolence was never mark'd more clear;
This figure, now his lamp delighted tries,
As if he saw some pleasing prospect rise:
What pity that a mind so form'd for bliss,
Our legend says, that happiness could miss;
Now be his lamp the object of your sight,
His hand, observe it, covers o'er one light;
As if some view he dreaded to receive,
But nought unneedful would the Hermit give;
If mercy and reward were all his view,
He found temptations that could those subdue:
Alcestes view'd them with a moment's pause,
And to the legend their attention draws:

And now of Herman's sons so lov'd,
  The youngest but remain'd:
All that obedient to him prov'd,
  Or the bright mansion gain'd.

And well he might obtain the prize,
  Who mark'd his guide with care ;
And saw the blissful prospect rise,
  And saw the dreadful snare.

And now my friends, Alcestes says once more,
The paintings let us yet again explore :
One figure still perhaps is unobserv'd,
And pleasing hope for that we have reserv'd ;
The whole expression of this face you see,
Is soften'd by a sweet humility ;
And here the painter, master of his art,
Displays the very movements of his heart.
Revered Alphonso ! here thy love is seen,
For me thy pencil traced this moral scene ;
To these he fixed my mind with early care,
And bid me place my guardian safety there ;
There, warnings to my youth, these scenes have
    brought,
There, lessons to the young my age has taught.

Observe this lamp with both its lights display'd,
With care you see this figure seems to tread ;
In every winding dreadful gulphs are seen,
The onward path leads to yon glorious scene.

Enough our honour'd friend ! the brothers cry,
Thy generous purpose we can well apply ;

The glowing tints speak from that striking scene,
A lesson that shall point thy wish within ;
Strong but in weakness, in our strength most weak,
Our conscious weakness, now these aids would seek ;
More diffident our course of virtue run,
And chuse the lamp of Herman's youngest son.

TO DELIA.

FADE thy leaves thou beauteous rose,
In those sweet scenes which thee disclose?
And droops thy head thou lily fair,
Declining in the balmy air?

Then take your beauty's transient power,
Ye pageants of a summer's hour:
And if there be yet aught more frail,
Give it to the passing gale.

Can brilliant gems, can glittering ore,
My Delia's health or peace restore?
Thy treasures back, oh earth! receive,
Or blindly still let fortune give.

How weak the pride of grandeur's sway!
Since all are born of equal clay;

G

Vainly alike we place our trust,
In noble or in servile dust.

Think not my Delia beauty's charm,
Could guard thy growing years from harm,
Or teach misfortune's pensive brow,
With conscious dignity to glow.

Be mental worth my Delia's care,
Unfading charm ! divinely fair !
Oh may its spell with potent ray,
Thro' youth and age direct thy way.

And take, oh take ! th' instructive page,
Which wisdom gives for every age ;
So shall thy richly polish'd mind,
Collect its treasures unconfin'd.

My Delia ! see for noble blood,
Thy words be gentle, actions good :
Let all thy thoughts exalted be,
And virtue thy nobility.

Then at devotion's hallow'd shrine,
Give every grace a seal divine ;
For prayers and deeds united rise,
To Heaven the richest sacrifice.

If prosperous scenes shall thee surround,
These be thy valued treasures found;
While fair humility shall reign,
A guardian o'er the heavenly train.

But, if thy tide of joys run low,
And friends with happier day should go,
Still mistress o'er thyself be seen,
And let thy virtues hail thee queen !

THE BIRTH DAY

THREE YOUNG LADIES,

O'ER times and seasons, days and years,
    The muses keep a watchful eye,
Deceive the conq'ring hand of time,
    And what they love forbid to die,

TO ELIZA.

The sage may say your blooming cheek,
    Shall with its sister roses fade :

TO SALLY.

Your sparkling eye it's lustre lose,
    And future years it's beauties shade.

TO HELEN.

Your wit, that now with potent charm,
  Invites our hearts to frolic mirth,
Sink blunted by the edge of time,
  And lose the fire which gave it birth.

Let sacred friendſhip still inspire,
  Still shall they flourish in my song,
Eliza's cheek shall always bloom,
  , And Helen's fire burn ever strong.

Still shall the Muses hail the day,
  Which to their aid the graces sent,
For uncouth were the rugged rhyme,
  If they no genial polish lent.

Propitious fortune ! smile this day,
  And hear the friend and poet's prayer,
Be these, thro' every scene of life,
  The darling objects of thy care.

And may this welcome day's return,
  With thy best favors still be crown'd,
And ever shining with the rest,
  Be rosy health and virtue found.

SONNET.

NOW dark December's gloom is gone,
　　Then go with it corroding care;
With festive mirth and jocund song,
　　To hail the rising year prepare.

Let beauty wear its gayest robe,
　　While wit exerts its brightest powers,
Let all within your breast be May,
　　And peace and joy shall lead your hours.

Tho' wint'ry storms may still descend,
　　And snow may whiten o'er the ground,
Yet hope presents yon smiling spring,
　　And rising beauty blooms around.

See from the zephyr's balmy wing,
  Propitious health her roses shed,
To meet her in the morning breeze,
  Shall tempt you from your drowsy bed.

Now dark December's gloom is gone,
  And go with it corroding care;
With festive mirth and jocund song,
  To hail the rising year prepare.

SONNET.

HOW blest the hours! when Celia's voice,
    Would calm my anxious cares to rest,
Could make my drooping heart rejoice,
    And kindle hope within my breast.
Ah! hours alas, for ever flown,
    Ah! scenes enjoy'd no more,
Yet say, has wealth aught happier known,
    Or found a richer store.

Ah! hours where bright content was seen,
    Unclouded sunshine of the mind!
Where friendship left no void within,
    Nor own'd a thought it wish'd confin'd.
The eye there beam'd its joy around,
    The tongue was love and truth,
And there was frolic humour found,
    And fancy, child of youth.

SONNET.

THE peaceful joys which virtue gives,
  She gives without allay,
Hoped, recollected, or enjoy'd,
  They gild life's brightest day.

Ye peaceful shades ! ye flowery lawns !
  Ye streams which murmur by !
'Tis innocence which makes your charms
  So grateful to the eye.

And ye, who trace the blue expanse,
  Or sport upon the green,
Sweet sympathy attracts my mind,
  With you to taste the scene.

Then piety and friendship pure,
  And soft benevolence,
Improve to me whate'er of good,
  Kind Heaven shall here dispense.

SONNET.

BUT now—and hope to fancy's eye
  Her blooming garlands spread,
And opening to my eager sight,
  Their vivid tints display'd;
But ah! deceitful and unkind,
She gives them to an adverse wind,
  Nor heeds a suppliant's grief;
From thee alas! capricious power,
Vainly would sorrow pluck a flower,
  Or picture a relief.

Reason perhaps, with looks severe,
  Shall make me this reply,
Thy passions are those adverse storms,
  That wait thy victory.
Subdue the thoughts which folly share,
Subsided lie each anxious care,
  And when thy work is done,
Contented with an humble lot,
Lie down, forgetting and forgot,
  Beneath some simple stone.

TO ELIZA S——.

———

THE weary traveller tired with roaming,
   Homeward turns his willing feet,
Kindest, friendliest counsel giving,
   If a stranger he should meet.

Heaven speed thy journey gentle stranger,
   Thine's a road which I have gone,
Think not my friendship too presuming,
   If its dangers I make known.

A pleasant hill now lies before thee,
   Mind to keep the middle way,
Danger in pleasing forms shall 'tice thee,
   Lure thee from thy path to stray.

But a faithful guide attending,
   Thou'lt discern each specious foe,

And her unerring glass presenting,
  Shews they lead to lasting woe.

Vainly may pleasure seek to tempt thee,
  Tho' with flowers her path be spread,
Thy guide can see her vot'ries hasting,
  To the mansions of the dead.

Some, you'll observe intemperance leading,
  To her bowers of cloying sweets,
But from behind yon ghastly figures,
  Drag them to their fell retreats.

Her crowns of poppies ease may offer,
  On down intreat thee to repose;
But in th' inglorious lake oblivion,
  All her votaries she throws.

There too sink those led by folly,
  And dissipation's giddy train,
Nor those whom vanity is leading,
  Can her empty gifts retain.

As towards the summit thou'rt ascending,
  Other foes shall thee surround,
Be sure to keep a steady footing,
  It is all enchanted ground.

To her high lands ambition tempts thee,
  Shews thee grandeur's envied state :
Believe it all a fair delusion.
  Wretched are her followers fate.

Some she leads o'er seas tempestuous,
  Sink beneath the foaming waves,
Others, from dreadful heights she plunges,
  Find below untimely graves.

From all these foes thy guide shall save thee,
  Pleasant may'st thou find the road,
Innocence thy fair attendant,
  To bright wisdom's blest abode.

Prosperous be thy journey, stranger,
  Thine's a road I well have known ;
Nor think my friendship too presuming,
  If its dangers I have shewn.

TO ———.

TILL life shall cease t' inform this mould'ring clay,
The soft affections round my heart will play;
Still must I feel, for so the Fates ordain,
Nor can one adverse blast be spent in vain;
But hope, e'en now, would shew me brighter hours,
Inventive fancy deck her chosen bowers;
Beneath the sky prepare some clime serene,
And bid each gentle virtue guard the scene;
There tender friendship's animating ray,
Without one selfish passion's base allay;
And health, and peace, and genius she bestows,
And all the fairyland with pleasure glows;
The Muses, Loves, and Graces, sport around,
No pain or sorrow treads the hallow'd ground;
Delusion all—reason denies her aid,
Touches the landscape, and its beauties fade,
Thus spoke the tongue where earth too deeply
        charm'd,
Thus felt the heart by strong affections warm'd;
Let earth for brighter prospects be resign'd,
And firmer hope bestow a calmer mind.

TO THE SAME.

IF prosperous scenes should open on our way,
Friendship has charms to gild the happiest day,
And numerous griefs humanity may feel,
Her soothing power has suited balms to heal;
As she recedes, our energies subside,
And earth's gay scenes appear a languid void;
Thus drooping flowers when chill'd by midnight air,
Contraćt their leaves, and fold themselves with care;
But when the sun ascends to light the day,
They soon expand to catch the vital ray;
With animated vigour see them rise,
Beneath the azure of unclouded skies;
But, if the hollow winds and beating rain,
Sweep o'er the hills, and deluge on the plain;
Denied the genial beam which gave them birth,
They then unheeded sink to native earth.

ODE TO HOPE.

BRIGHT queen of care beguiling smiles
    Supreme in airy state ;
To draw the sting from fortune's wiles,
    And smooth the brow of fate.
Thine is the music of the spring,
Thy breath can freshest verdure bring,
    To dress the cheerless plain ;
When the hoarse tempest lawless roves,
And Autumn yields her golden groves,
    To Winter's dreary reign,

Thou canst the massy gates unbar
    That close on happy days,
The tides of woe when nations war,
    Thy steady anchor stays ;
Far as the beam of fancy flies,
Thy fair ideal kingdoms rise,
    And vernal garlands bloom ;
Nor breathes a wretch so lost to thee,
Who thro' thy power no gleam can see,
    That dawns on joy to come.

Fortune her splendid sons displays,
  An envied glittering train,
But ah ! the bliss that crowns their days
  Must still with thee remain.
Each take the sphere where each must move,
Nor sink below, nor rise above,
  Thy soft illusive voice ;
The varied wish of all who live,
Thy specious promises can give,
  Unbounded as their choice.

In thee youth's golden dreams acquired
  A fair but faithless friend,
By reason's sober hand attired,
  My future steps attend.
Those gay delusions ever fled,
Which unsubstantial forms had fed,
  Thy pallid sister shared ;
Her trembling hand she'd oft employ,
To scatter shades upon the joy,
  Which disappointment spared.

Come soothing power ! but more serene,
  Thy temper'd light display ;
I yield to fancy's giddy queen,
  Thy meteor's dazzling ray.

H

No more my ardent wishes rise
To solid good below the skies,
　　Or court delusive power ;
Yet cheer my paths if virtue treads,
Shine thro' the tear that sorrow sheds,
　　And sooth my dying hour.

WRITTEN AT W. C. IN OCTOBER,

AT SUN-SET.

GRATEFUL to me this calm retreat,
  By fond remembrance dear;
With joy I hail my rural seat,
  For peace and love were here.

From scenes more chang'd, as these I trace,
  To memory's records true:
Reflection throws a softer grace,
  O'er every rising view.

No more befriended by thy shade,
  Thou fast declining oak,
Our simple banquet shall be made,
  Or pass our harmless joke.

Ye rocks in antic forms ye rose,
　　And flowery garlands wore ;
But straying by your fringed brows,
　　I meet my friends no more.

Nor yon fantastic thorn beneath,
　　Their mossy seat I share ;
Or tread with them the velvet heath,
　　And gather flowerets there.

No more, regretted friends, to you,
　　The varied moss I bring;
Or craneberry, or berry blue,
　　From out the purple ling.

As yonder western heights between,
　　Deep floods of waters glide,
Rich autumn's painted skies are seen,
　　Reflected on their tide.

Nor charms alas ! delight their eyes,
　　This setting sun reveals ;
Tho' clear wild Cambria's mountains rise,
　　And Mona's magic hills.

Nor mirthful now they hear me say,
　　I trod that fairy ground,

And there with youthful elves so gay,
　Had danced the frolic round.

Now silvering Cloghow's sable vest,
　The full orb'd moon appears,
And on each floweret's tender breast,
　Hang sympathetic tears.

Declining autumn yields her sheaves,
　Ye fading scenes farewell!
I would return, with flowers and leaves,
　A while with you to dwell.

As winter would each charm deform,
　Thou overhanging rock;
Oh! from the ravage of the storm
　Defend my favorite oak.

Tho' cares perhaps, and grief I seek,
　Bid peace and you adieu;
What shakes the strong, may spare the weak
　And I revisit you.

AT THE SAME PLACE.

FROM all that hope and fear between
   Corroding cares employ,
I visit thee beloved scene,
   And give this day to joy.

From where the east yon mountains crown,
   To the smooth western sea,
Each view by summer gaily shown,
   The past endears to me.

For perfumed flowers now seated gay,
   Did here the cheerless train,
Of desolating winter stray,
   And bind with icy chain.

Her frigid hand would lose it's power,
   These beauties to erase ;
For the young charms of vernal hours,
   Fond memory would replace.

To innocence these scenes invite,
  The fragrant air is health ;
Unlike the dangerous delight,
  That waits on power and wealth.

The herd their flowery carpets share,
  And youthful gambols try ;
While the plum'd people of the air,
  Tune nature's general joy.

E'en rocks has this gay season drest,
  With garlands on their brow :
The world, too like a flinty breast,
  Lurks in a seemly show.

With youthful hue my favorite free,
  In slender robe array'd ;
Extends it's shade again to me,
  With thinner foliage spread.

Phebus withdraw that potent ray,
  To nobler conquests soar ;
Yield it the triumph of to day,
  And former day's restore.

Mr. GEORGE KENDAL,

Who was drowned upon his birth-day, and the day he
he had been bound apprentice.

———————

" Ah ! only shewn to check our fond pursuits,
" And teach our humbled hopes that life is vain !"

SWEET youth farewell ! the day that gave thee
    birth,
Again unites thee to thy parent earth ;
That day, to busy cares devoted thee,
That day, was crown'd with rest and liberty.
Soft be the slumbers of thy lowly bed,
And lightly lie the turf upon thy head ;
While from thy cold remains with mournful eye,
The muse collects the sweets which shall not die.

Pensive and sad she leaves her joyless bowers,
To strew thy early tomb with choicest flowers.
Tho' from thy cheek death pluck'd the blushing rose,
Thy rising virtues still its sweets disclose :
And oft as Flora paints the purple year,
Shall recollection trace thy emblem there.
When hopeful youth, or worth like thine shall fall,
The thoughts of thee for added tears shall call.
Our kindest wishes were in error sown,
Infinite wisdom gave thee joys unknown.
Fain would our languid spirits wing their way,
To hail thee in the realms of radiant day.
This warning lesson read ye gay and young,
Who thoughtless flutter in life's giddy throng.
Of health, of youth possest, still frail your breath,
For many are the hidden roads to death.

    Thus o'er the dust we love we fondly mourn,
And wait the voice that bids our dust return.
Loosen'd from earth, would reach yon upper sky,
By " faith, man's early immortality."
Thro' these afflictions push with vigour on,
Shoot the dark gulph, and seize a heavenly crown.

WIT AND JUDGMENT.

ON the wild margin of the flood,
An airy structure gaily stood.
Its smiling queen with easy air,
Amuses there the young and fair :
And homage takes from every quarter,
E'en from the peasant to the garter.
For glowing in her brightest hours,
She vies with beauty's mighty powers.
All court her graces, wish her name,
And Wit they call'd the shining dame.
As holy pilgrims always bear
Some relic to inspire their prayer,
So did the votaries of our queen
Joy in her favours to be seen.

Numerous were the gifts they bore,
Which in as varied modes were wore.
They took their hints from fancy's eye,
And shone with many a sparkling dye.
Promiscuous tho' they still were thrown,
Each was delighted with his own.
Eager their presents to display,
They all went satisfied away.
The Pedant shew'd his pun with glee.
The Beau his brilliant repartee.
And Ridicule, the Cynic's treasure,
Was lavish'd with unsparing measure:
Whilst mimickr'y, which all could fit,
Was valued as a gift from wit.
Various was the strange collection,
Where least studied, most perfection,
A medley odd of grave and gay,
That gleam'd around a sudden ray,
Which often by it's magic charm,
Grave reason quickly could disarm ;
Triumphant to the thoughtless eye,
They bore unquestion'd victory.
But when to judgment they were shewn,
Few of their beauties he would own ;
When tried by his dividing hand,
The false materials could not stand ;

His separating art display'd,
The lasting charm from fleeting shade;
The different value each should share,
And in the eye of reason bear.
Puns were a senseless play with words,
Which to no rule of taste accords;
A repartee a forward hit,
Sprung from impertinent conceit;
And ridicule had scarce a feature,
Which was not copied from ill-nature;
Envy and apathy 'twas plain,
Had form'd the scorpions in her train;
And not the slightest part was found,
To touch on philanthropic ground;
Whilst all the mimic's varied art,
Betray'd suspicions of his heart;
In others characters he shone,
Then most unmindful of his own;
From every weakness he display'd,
His errors took a deeper shade;
How cruel to the tenderer sense,
Was felt th' illiberal low pretence,
A laugh to raise or plaudit gain,
By aught that gave another pain.
Thus were Wit's favours oft inspected,
And their slight value soon detected;

That judgement paid her little deference,
And ever merited a preference,
Run in swift murmurs thro' the crowd,
By whispers that were something loud.
Her ears the grating truth had caught,
And tho' she was no friend to thought,
It piqued her pride, and rais'd her fear.
A formidable foe so near.
Her power she knew he still could foil,
Or open force or hidden wile.
Yet ere she yielded to despair,
She rais'd her voice in ardent prayer ;
Be every pitying power adored,
She said, and all their power implored,
If aught is in my origin,
Of ether pure or breath divine.
Sure some attendant spirit still,
Shall guard me from impending ill.
This equal aid be ever near.
Guardian ! Protector ! now appear,
Oh ! save me from my dreaded foe,
Who plans my kingdom's overthrow.
She ceas'd, and o'er the trembling dame,
Hover'd a gleam of lambent flame.
While soft enchantments held her soul,
These cheering words her fears control ;

Behold around the vivid ray,
That gave thee to the light of day,
When negatives shall well restore *
The subtle essence of thy power,
Soaring above the low and vain,
E'en wisdom shall approve thy reign,
Then all inspiring thou shalt move
Judgement, thy native charms to love,
And from your union shall arise,
The brightest form beneath the skies.

Tho' he conveys no golden dower,
    Nor is with fortune seen,
He lights by his creative power,
    A brighter world within ;
The busy hours successive come,
With their enriching stores to bloom,
    In intellectual light ;
While he for ever bright and young,
Displays them in his magic song,
    An ever new delight.

Adown the stream of following years,
    The world's gay votaries pass,
Distinction vainly interferes,
    To mark the common mass ;

---

* " 'Tis not a tale, 'tis not a jest,
   " Admir'd with laughter at a feast."
                                    COWLEY.

When earth resumes the dust she gave,
The sons of genius from the grave,
  Protracted life shall gain.
For undepress'd and unconfin'd,
The tuneful ardour of the mind,
  Shall catch the breath of fame.

My last VISIT to W--Y C--G,

ON THE

SICKNESS of Mrs. W--Y.

———

SCENES long belov'd! for ever dear!
  If aught of music in my tongue,
Your beauties thro' the varied year,
  Have tun'd my sweetest song.
When infant spring brought budding flowers,
And summer sat in perfum'd bowers,
  In autumn's changing face,
The snows that crown'd yon mountain's brow,
And storms that stirr'd the wave below,
  Gave but sublimer grace.

Here oft my harmless childhood play'd,
　Traced the bright insect on its wing ;
Thro' these wild scenes delighted stray'd,
　With innocence and spring.
My youthful heart would oft employ,
Bright hope to dress my future joy,
　As here it sported round ;
Smiled with me in my walks along,
Cheer'd me in nature's artless song,
　And in yon cot was found.

The stranger's home ! the traveller's rest
　Where Want could never long complain,
The tale there melted Pity's breast,
　The rich had heard in vain.
Ah Spring ! that nature calls to live,
Could'st thou her faded form revive,
　Who could for misery feel,
Who rich alone in bounty's power,
Would spread around her little store,
　And share her simple meal.

There oft the infant brood I brought,
　Rescued from savage plunderer's hand,
Till plumed, by native instinct taught,
　They join'd the tuneful band.

I

Farewell! thou hospitable dome!
My frequent and my happiest home,
 No more in thee to dwell;
No more this fragrant air to breathe,
Or sleep this friendly roof beneath,
 Ah! can I say—Farewell!

ON THE DEATH OF

A YOUNG GENTLEMAN.

LET no unhallowed step approach the tomb,
 Sacred to spotless innocence and truth ;
The fragrant rose here waved her vermeil bloom,
 And gentlest manners grac'd the glow of youth.

When bright Aurora lights the blushing east,
 When the mild zephyrs meet the scorching ray,
No tint more beauteous can Aurora caft,
 No breath more gentle, fans the god of day.

The gather'd fragrance of the vernal year,
 The softest harmony that wakes the grove,
Nor steals the sense, nor charms th' enraptur'd ear,
 Like wisdom rising with the form we love.

Our ardent wishes strip the wing of time,
    To give each portion what the world calls good,
Health, riches, honor, but a changing clime
    Presents us storms and death's unsparing flood.

Here oft as friendship drops the falling tear,
    The Muse shall spread instruction from this tomb,
Shall warn the young that death is ever near*,
    For in the morning did the master come.

Yet while we mourn the fall of this fair flower,
    Faith gives to hope her animating ray :
Pierces the cloud which veils that glorious hour,
    When all our light afflictions pass away.

---

* Mark xiii, 35.

Mrs. MIRIAM GILLISON.

AS those we dearly love resign their breath,
Living we taste the bitterness of death,
And while life hovers o'er the languid frame,
Plead the strong tie to fan th' expiring flame;
Reluctant to the tomb their clay we trust,
And moisten with our tears the silent dust;
Chain'd to this earth our weak ideas lie,
Nor trace the spirit to its native sky.

Much honor'd shade forgive this falling tear,
The selfish sorrow that could wish thee here,
From every mortal care securely free,
Thou ne'er shalt feel what now is felt for thee.

Death fixed his seal and stamp'd thy virtues true,
Thy life's fair page the faithful Muse would view,
And there religion spread a pleasing charm ;
Pure as its precepts as its prospects warm :
There soft compassion met the tale of grief,
And ere 'twas ask'd, bestow'd the wish'd relief;
How lov'd how valu'd in each social tye,
Witness the falling tear, the heart-felt sigh :
Thus lov'd, thus mourn'd, our comforts pass away,
Till death discloses a celestial day.

Mrs. ANNE GILLISON.

———————

THE deep-toned bell arrests my listening ear,
And pensive sadness shades the opening year ;
Chain'd to a bed of languor, and of pain,
My lyre untuned has lost its wonted strain.
Yet all its trembling strings o'er Anna's urn,
Again would vibrate, with my heart would mourn.
Friend of the good, farewell ! my friend adieu !
The heart you often cheer'd, must mourn for you,
Ever was seen your hospitable door,
Opening to cheer the friendless, feed the poor.
Oft on my solitary hours this knell,
By brooding fancy heard, shall sound—farewell !
Where adulation sooths a rising name,
The comment marks perhaps a dubious aim,

But from the tomb be cold suspicion fled,
No pity melts, or flattery sooths the dead.
So freed—to virtue and affection true,
The mourning muse this finish'd course would view,
For points contending be the bigot found,
Declaring zeal and resting in a sound.
Truths uncontested here could force impart
To stamp the Christian's duties on the heart.
Benevolence thence gave her open smile,
Sincerity her tongue that spake no guile ;
Forgiveness there thro' transient anger shone,
The heart that free from harm, suspected none,
The tears of wealth in smiles of ease may end,
But ah ! when poverty has lost a friend,
Remembrance, that in prosperous days may sleep,
Must with the sick and poor sad vigils keep.
Grateful to feeling hearts and friendly eyes,
Oh quickly let the sheltering pile arise*,
Where misery most forlorn for years to come,
Skreen'd from the world's contempt, shall find a
      home.
When winter rages, there in future days,
Rever'd tradition shall repeat her praise.

---

* Alluding to a charitable institution, endowed by Mrs Ann Gillison.

While round their blazing fires these sit and tell,
What they have heard of her who built that cell.
Ambitious each to rescue from the grave,
How good she was, what charities she gave;
By faithful records shall her memory shine,
And still fresh olives round the cypress twine.

Minist'ring angels of the grace of Heaven,
To you ye poor, the rich and good were given :
If faithful thus, their treasures they employ,
Your present comfort yields their future joy.
When at the voice of All-commanding Power,
What braved the wreck of time shall be no more;
And in one general ruin shall resolve,
" This globe, and all which it inherit shall dissolve."
Unfading honors then, and joys unknown,
Which clouds of witnesses for them have sown.
Shall He, whose bright example they pursued,
With these approving words reward imperfect good;
" I was an hungred and ye gave me bread."—

MEMORY OF A LADY,

Whom the Author much esteemed when very young.

———

IF gratitude was e'er a debt,
  Or friendship were a tye,
Then will I think on Margaret,
  Till I shall droop and die.

To me succeeding years have shewn,
  Thou wert a peerless maid ;
For years alas ! are past and gone,
  Since thou in dust wert laid.

The hours of folly, light and vain,
  I count a loss to me ;
But pleasures in reflection's train,
  Are those I pass'd with thee.

To follow thy engaging worth,
  My early days inclin'd ;
And now I fondly call them forth,
  To cheer my pensive mind.

Not dearer to my youthful heart,
  My early fancy's pride,
Than now, when sicken'd hopes depart,
  And pleasing scenes subside.

How oft the time I would prolong,
  When listening to thy tongue ;
For who with wisdom lived so long,
  That ever died so young.

THE BIRTH of GENIUS.

ANALYSIS OF THE BIRTH OF GENIUS.

Genius, the offspring of Judgement and Wit, is attended at his birth by the Power who instills virtuous dispositions, and by the liberal endowments of Nature : also by the Sciences, who enrich him with their gifts. As he advances in life, he is instructed in the proper use of them. A preceptor becoming necessary, Pleasure and Assiduity offer themselves. The mother prefers the first, the father the second. The mother, though defeated in her intention, contrives to place her son under the influence of Pleasure; in consequence of which, he is lost for a time to every good purpose; but on the repentance of the parents, the justice of the Divine Being restores their son, who, placed under the care of Assiduity, arrives at the excellence of his nature.

GENIUS and learning tho' we gain,
Genius and learning bless in vain ;
How shared with error and with woe,
The progress of my tale would shew,
Till application call'd them forth,
And virtue gives its labours worth.

A pair of heavenly origin,
O'er empire once were born to shine;
The king received from Jove's high hand,
His skill profound, his just command;
And from a ray of ether's flame,
The queen deriv'd her dazzling frame.
One child they had alone to bless,
With hopes of an extended race.
To hail the stranger's dawning hours,
Assembled all the gifted powers:
As rank prescrib'd they now resort,
And first, Carmenta paid her court.
I come, she said, oh! most rever'd,
Accept the offering I've prepar'd;
The brilliant presents others give
From mine shall higher worth receive.
Behold! this phial's limpid juice,
In every scene of sovereign use.

From the pure lily's virgin breast,
    I charm'd the chrystal dew,
The beam which first Aurora drest,
    As faithfully I drew.

With these a zephyr's breath infus'd,
    Then pierc'd the briny wave;
And thence, this beauteous pearl produc'd,
    From Ocean's richest cave.

While thus to form and more refine,
  I heavenly fire impell'd,
Within my essence I confine,
  Hermetically seal'd.

This essence still from chance secure,
  No time or use shall waste;
And prayers shall best extract it pure,
  And leave its fountain chaste.

As other graces issue forth,
  To raise the prince's name,
My gift conveys them richer worth,
  And yields them pure to fame.

The next the prince's birth had drawn,
To hail with gifts his early dawn;
Advanced with step of easy grace,
And half unveil'd her lovely face;
While beauteous flowers adorn'd her head,
A sun was on her breast display'd.
A cabinet and key she bore,
And thus set forth her offer'd store:
While freely all the gifted train,
Adorn your offspring, bless your reign,
My works which have for ages been,
And yet, alas! but dimly seen,

And careless view'd by common sight,
My works, this key display to light :
And if applied with skilful hand,
By these five doors my stores command..
This door unfolded, charms the sight.
From this the powers of sound delight.
Here Flora has her perfumes drest.
And here Pomona meets the taste.
But ah ! the fifth essay with care,
Angels, or fiends inhabit there.
From this my works their worth receive :
Here it expires, or here shall live.
Here lives offence ! here high reward !
Carmenta's phial is your guard !

The next an endless scroll had brought.
The next a vase with wonder wrought,
Form'd to receive and to produce,
Amazing stores to instant use.

These gifts insured the royal pair.
A joy disdaining fear to share ;
They scarcely call'd in Hope to see,
The honours of their progeny.
E'en now around his infant frame,
The beams of future glory flame ;
Yet of the fates they wish'd to know,
The happy future sanction'd now.

Sanguine, they strike their magic rod,
To draw them from their dark abode;
Where far removed from mortal ken,
Decrees of gods they write for men :
Their brazen pens, their juices lave,
From Cocytus's inky wave;
And straight th' irrevocable word,
On adamantine leaves record.
With wond'rous skill the distaff's wound,
And soon the wheel of life goes round;
The sheers suspend, the thread is spun,
Tis cut—and mortal life is done.
The royal pair these prayers repeat,
To draw them from their awful seat;
Dread sisters of the rosy hours,
Daughters of Jove! relentless powers!
Who write with an eternal pen,
The firm decree of gods on men,
Sisters three, enrob'd in white,
Appear, and sanction our delight.
Ascend, and from your dark abodes,
Shew us the bright decrees of Gods :
And lo! dark clouds obscure the night,
With semblance premature of night.
Tempest succeeds the Zephyr's breeze,
And troubled waves to glassy seas :
Confusion thunders thro' the skies,
And stern the destinies arise.

Earth cleaves, and, at their near approach,
Fair Order shudders from their touch.

Tell us, they cry, why we muſt rise,
To trouble earth and vex the skies;
While we by partial call are staid,
The work of worlds remains delay'd;
Summon'd by you we yet are come,
Then hear our words, for they are doom't
The Prince, from many potent pow'rs,
Has brilliant gifts to gild his hours;
But all is vain they might display,
If shorten'd life forbid their stay;
And ah! his wheel of life appears
Inclin'd to stop at eighteen years;
But ere our work decisive prove,
Still we must join in hate and love;
If firm the thread of life shall keep,
The wheel may stop, death is but sleep,
And even from that sleep to free,
Admits of possibility;
But circumstance will so obtain,
That scarce a ray from hope we gain,
One hint observe and well receive,
(All alas that we can give;)
Virtuous pursuits wait glorious ends,
And much depends on choice of friends.

K

Hastening th' attendant shades away,
This said, they quit the glare of day;
Ghastly they smiled, their torch they fir'd,
And with the jar of elements retir'd.

For shades, shines Phoebus' radiant beam,
And what the niggard fates scarce deem,
As possible to human skill,
Hope enters ready to fulfil.
A thousand schemes their minds prepare,
Sanguine in each to shun the snare.

Their orders issue thro' the land,
And all the wise before them stand ;
The mystic presents to explain,
That nought might be bestow'd in vain ;
These give Carmenta's gift it's force,
And shew religion virtue's source :
All other means prove insecure,
To leave it safe and draw it pure.

The Cabinet they next explore,
Of various charms, a wondrous store ;
From the first door to vision rise,
What natures curious hand supplies ;
Expanding all the wond'ring sense,
To beauty and benevolence ;
And here—the masters skill'd to teach,
Explain what human pow'rs can reach.

The fine gradations far they see,
Till lost in vast infinity.
Immense, till distance fhades their light,
Minute, they lessen from the sight;
The second door unfolds to cheer
With pleasing sounds th' enraptur'd ear;
Here intercourse, its bliss receives,
And heav'nly conversation lives;
Nor here the master's skill is less,
The force of language to impress;
Than wake the sounds that touch the heart,
And all their pow'r to charm impart,
The two succeeding doors display,
What lib'ral nature can convey.
Our pleasures with our wants can sort,
And lure us to our own support;
And ever faithful to her rights,
From harm repels, to good incites.
The masters shew the prudent care,
That ought these bounteous gifts to share;
And punishment she will exert,
O'er those who waste or who pervert.

The skilful masters next unroll
The windings of the awful scroll,
And teach, tho' earth her dust will claim,
Deeds shall retain their place in fame;

And actions, vicious or sublime,
Shall live accurs'd, or blest, thro' time.

Next, the internal world they view,
And there their pupils' wonder drew,
And more minutely to explore,
Open the last, th' important door ;
It they approach with sacred awe,
And first Carmenta's phial draw,
Whose sacred essence can refine,
All mortal gift by aid divine ;
Then, straight they touch those springs to wake,
From which all deeds their merit take,
Above cold maxims, there they shew,
The generous act exalted glow ;
Here precept takes its force to warm,
And virtues wear a living charm ;
For faint assent, here faith has given,
To ardent hope her absent heaven ;
For forms here warm devotions* rise,
To wrest the blessing from the skies ;

---

* Devotion, that can bind th' Almighty's arm,
And of its thunder his right hand disarm,
She passes quick Heav'ns lofty chrystal walls,
And the high gates fly open when she calls;
Her voice did once the sun's swift chariot stay,
And on the verge of Heav'n held back the day,

BLACKMORE.

Here justice melts at mercy's charms,
And guilt by penitence disarms ;
For tardy alms cold duties guide,
Here nameless charities reside ;
Here tenderest sympathies are found,
And nature seals her firmest bond ;
By these, impell'd to deeds of fame,
The hero spreads his awful name,
The sacred guardians of the land,
'Tis here that patriot minds expand;
Where human laws are weak to bind,
Here sense of honour leads the mind,
'Tis Liberty, 'tis nature's school,
Where virtue's unconfin'd to rule ;
And here arise those arts with grace,
Which learning is so proud to dress;
Beyond the critic line she draws,
Here warm imagination glows ;
Her rules may harmony impart,
Here rise the sounds that warm the heart.

Sweet poetry ! the charm is thine,
That here the sister arts combine ;
And here deserve thy tripple wreathe,
Where music speaks, and paintings breathe;
And let th' according chaplet be,
Inscrib'd to heav'nly harmony ;

For Liberty and Nature's school,
Teach graces unattain'd by rule.

The prince was quickly skill'd to reach,
Th' extent of all that art could teach ;
To each he gave a master's claim,
And for a trophy sign'd his name ;
And soon their easy task was o'er,
For Learning could inform no more.

The parents, with exulting strains,
Declare a friend alone remains ;
And early there their care shall be,
And well observ'd their far decree,
That all who can adorn a court,
From earth's far peopl'd climes resort,
That for their son with high reward,
They choose a friend his youth to guard;
The oracle they thus pursu'd,
And hop'd their evil fate subdu'd,
Among the first resorting there,
Two equally divide their care ;
Tutor'd by fashion and by art,
One won the queen's consenting heart;
The other, veil'd by modesty,
Yet gain'd the king's approving eye ;
The first, with self-assuring mein,
Gaily approach'd the brilliant queen;

No diffidence her claims prevent,
No aukward fears produced restraint;
By art, with lilies vied her neck,
And borrow'd roses stain'd her cheek,
With soften'd voice, and studied smiles,
She thus the easy queen beguiles—

You spoke your wishes, charming queen,
And lo! th' accomplish'd world are seen.
So with the first my claims are brought,
And more than all, with justice fraught;
The hours of joy bright queen are mine,
And 1 with youth and beauty shine;
No drudging labour can oppress,
Whenever I am call'd to bless;
Perhaps your Lord, by means severe,
Will try to shun the fate you fear;
With joy repelling eye will blast,
The time of pleasure youth should taste.
If there thou yield, thy son with grief,
Will court his fate as wish'd relief;
Steady, a kindred pow'r defend,
In me fair queen protect a friend.

Her polish'd grace the queen approv'd,
And thought a kindred pow'r she lov'd,
One that could fortune's gifts employ,
To brighten every hour with joy.

Vainly the king she would ensnare,
For him, her words dissolv'd in air;
His modest suppliant he view'd,
Who silent yet before him stood;
An hour-glass in her hand she bore,
An amaranth in her hair she wore,
But doubtful by her dress display'd,
Its folds were form'd of light and shade;
She stood thus dubious in her worth,
Waiting till Judgment call'd her forth;
Nor, till a favouring look she caught,
Own'd the pretensions she had brought;
And then in words of simple frame,
She thus advanc'd her modest claim—

I have no brilliant parts to boast,
Nor was I train'd with art or cost;
I seldom with the gay am seen,
The great dislike my humble mien;
But those who have me most carest;
Will say I grateful am at least;
And own thro' me it was they shone,
And tell of wonders I have done;
By you directed, mighty lord,
Wonders again they shall record;
No lazy spell infests the ground,
Where I am lov'd and I am found;

If your protection I may ask,
To guard from evil be my task.

Friendship unchang'd resides above,
And there alone dwells equal love ;
While other blessings strew our road,
Faith points to these as promis'd good ;
E'en wedlock may this evil share,
And Wit and Judgment sometimes jar.
Our monarchs, tho' of heav'nly birth,
Must here partake the lot of earth ;
Their different tastes opinion guides,
An interest dear their heart divides ;
Their counsels each themselves obey,
And leave disputes to vulgar clay.

Invested with supreme command,
Which open force could ne'er withstand,
The king with public honours grac'd,
And near his son his favorite plac'd ;
To her confided all his stores,
And named her guardian of his hours.

The queen these counsels did not share
And opposition would not dare ;
In wiles she trusted for her cause,
To render vain the monarch's laws ;

To give persuasion to her tongue,
She tun'd her favorite's syren song;
If flattering praise could not secure,
She dazzling interest gave to lure;
Luxuriant charms around her spread,
With her own roses crown'd her head,
And all seducing to command,
With honour's palms she grac'd her hand;
In each some lurking spell there lay,
Potent to charm and to betray;
The first alluring as she draws,
She baited with the world's applause;
Then specious as the theme she sung,
The syren song flow'd from her tongue;
Virtue she sung a cheating dream;
High sounding honours were her theme;
She sung, that names thro' time rever'd,
Thro' toils and death had madly err'd;
Her grateful palms she then display'd,
A meed for favorites fortune made;
These too enchanting snares she spread,
Her soft temptations artful laid,
To draw the Prince to leave the bound,
Which Judgment fix'd to safety's ground,
No orisons now pierce the skies,
For aught Carmenta's gift supplies;
Its gay exterior all its merit,
Its form alone without its spirit.

And now the pride of all his store,
The prince but as a bauble wore;
A trinket, taking reputation,
As pearls of price were gems of fashion ;
And led by that capricious guide,
Thrown by the changing mode aside.

Often the prince now pass'd the bound,
His father gave to safety's ground;
Lost to the pow'r which should defend,
His guardian is no more a friend;
Nor doubtful longer she appears,
All sable is the robe she wears.

'Twere endless here to name the train,
That took from hence a mortal stain ;
Grant them the boon, forgot to lie,
Remember'd, it were infamy.

Needful supply for luxury's food,
The charms of interest next subdu'd ;
The hoards of avarice stood display'd,
Gaily the golden stores were spread :
There cheerless nature sunk in gloom,
'Twas virtue and affection's tomb ;
There nought of value now remains,
In aught the cabinet contains ;

For sordid interest's transient claim,
He sold the glories of his name.

Oh avarice ! were thy deeds forgot,
'Twould save humanity a blot ;
Peru nor Mexico should tell,
India or Africa reveal ;
Hide in the silence of the grave ;
Passions which nature never gave.
The injurer and the injur'd sleep,
Let memory then no vigils keep;
Oblivion ! their foul deeds receive,
But ah ! condemn'd by fame they live ;
History unsparing tells thro' time,
The savage wonders of their crime.

By pleasure's fascinating pow'r,
The rosy garland next he wore ;
No more he visits safety's ground,
No guardian for his hours is found;
His mother's favorite takes the reins,
And binds him in her pleasing chains ;
Silky and soft, and ting'd with gold,
But there was magic in their mold ;
Than adamantine bonds more strong,
To hold the hapless captive long ;
Their pow'r resistless they impart,
The mind to crush and bind the heart;

Furies that into storms awake,
For influence dread dominion take;
Chaos of elemental strife!
Here work your tragedies of life.

If to that fatal scene she lead,
I would not with my favorite tread ;
Let darkness veil its kindred scene,
Unseen the horrors wrought within;
Dread gulfs are hid in fairy bowers,
And poisons lurk in beauteous flowers ;
Who near their precincts dare to stray,
Contagions meet, or wild dismay.
There nothing curious be my choice,
To shun the daring forms of vice ;
But some unaw'd your haunts shall view,
And mark that vengeance dwells with you ;
With gifts most meet for actions foul,
Her worms of conscience for the soul ;
If error's labyrinth I must show,
Thro' scenes less guilty let me go ;
Not interest fell, nor vain applause,
Nor where tempestuous passion draws,
But rather where the drowsy sense,
Is lull'd by pamper'd indolence ;
There sunk in unaspiring ease,
I mourn my favorite lost to please ;

No good or ill incites his powers,
Lost to the guardian of his hours;
He festive wreathes alone desires,
Whose magic, damps his nobler fires;
Their sweets his senses all compose,
While music its soft aid bestows;
The goblet fair and downy couch,
Thus with his threaten'd fate approach;
Languid—scarce moves life's lazy thread,
It ceases now, the wheel is staid,
Unbroken firm, the thread to keep,
The wheel is stay'd, and death is sleep.

Reclin'd upon an ebon throne,
The drowzy god whom poppies crown,
Receives him in his silent shade,
With hanging juniper o'erspread;
The lizard and the dormouse there,
Forget the rigour of the year;
Around them lulling vapours rise,
From incense, mortals' sacrifice,
Attracting vapours to renew,
The cowslip and the mandrake's dew;
Clouds wrought in twilight's doubtful doom,
Inclose the borders of the gloom;
Nor moon's calm beam, nor sun's bright ray,
There draw the herald of the day;

But oft the beetle wheels around,
And there the moping owl is found.

The royal pair here weeping turn,
And past divisions deeply mourn ;
They own the justice of their fate,
And mercy thus they supplicate—

As error and distress are ours,
Be pardon yours Almighty powers ;
And while our humble prayers we pour,
And all your Providence adore,
If past offence we may repair,
To our repentance, oh ! declare !

Mercy remitting sorrow's date,
Thus answers by relenting fate—

For crimes be true repentance yours,
And for repentance pardon ours.
Tho' won by penitential tears,
She melts the sternness which he wears ;
Mercy thus potent to subdue,
Were weak not join'd by justice too ;
Attend the mandate of the skies,
So may your humbled hopes arise ;
For you bright queen to heaven allied,
Be duty to your Lord your guide ;

Where those would lead who should obey,
Disorders rule for equal sway ;
You sire who boast celestial birth,
Jove's mighty attribute on earth,
'Tis yours to clear the misty way,
And lead your son to life and day ;
Directed by your mighty powers,
Recall the guardian of his hours :
To execute th' important scheme,
Her labor lightly she shall deem ;
Tis yours to seal her doubtful worth,
And well instructed send her forth ;
For ere the wheel of life goes round,
Some worthy offering must be found.

He ceas'd, and well his words imprest,
An ardour in the monarch's breast ;
His hasten'd step he instant bent,
To trace the path his favorite went ;
He saw her on a rock reclin'd,
Where persevering ivy twin'd ;
And as an hour-glass now she turn'd,
Its wasting sands she deeply mourn'd.
Soon as the king appear'd in view,
Her garments lost their sable hue :
For as the shades dispell'd by light,
The black dissolv'd in spotless white.

Soon as the king her eye had caught,
A sprig of amaranth she brought;
And wav'd it with triumphant air,
And plac'd it in her flowing hair;
Whilst prostrate at his feet she fell,
Her artless words her raptures tell;
Prostrate she says—hail mighty Lord!
By you neglected I have err'd,
Oh guide me that I may restore,
The Prince whose loss we all deplore;
The creeping ivy climbs to height,
And insects lofty trees invite.
Deeds impossible to thought,
Are by application wrought;
By you directed mighty Lord,
Wonders again they shall record.

Her worth neglected touch'd his heart,
Relenting thoughts these words impart.
Thy pardon give and mine receive,
Cherish'd by me in future live;
Me to decree the gods inspire,
Thee they endow with active fire;
With winged feet then speed thy skill
To gain the summit of the hill.
Twelve sisters, sent on high import,
(The shining nymphs of Phœbus' court;)

L

Move in swift succession there,
Swift as they move, oh ! watch with care ;
Ardent the aid of each implore,
For ah ! they will return no more.

The monarch ceas'd, and while the sound
Yet vibrates in the air around,
She flew with more than mortal speed,
Over the intervening mead.
And soon she gains th' important hill,
Chosen her trials to fulfil ;
No more, she says, my weaken'd sense
Is lull'd by charms of indolence,
Nor driv'n by guilt to misery ;
Yet worse than useless shall I be,
For judgment now decides my worth,
And leads me to call genius forth.

Essaying then the rising ground,
Twelve nymphs of heav'nly form she found ;
And fair they were, of heav'nly show,
And locks of gold stray'd o'er their brow ;
Their locks of gold, they wav'd in air,
And tears bedew'd their faces fair ;
With varied hues each garment shines,
Their girdles shew'd the circling signs ;
And short their dress, and fleet their course,
Not stay'd by courtesy or force.

Oh nymph divine! our heroine cry'd,
That heed me not but onward glide,
To mortals sure your errands be,
And each some treasure has for me.

Mortal attend, they quick return'd,
For not unsought our gifts are earn'd:
Let every trifling thought give place,
And strive to conquer, in thy race.
They said, and bid the fair pursue,
In swift succession as they flew.
Then Application quick pursued;
Temptations nobly she subdued;
Tho' indolence her downy bed,
And pleasure, flaunting roses spread.—

The steady nymph disdainful ey'd
Their tempting sweets, and thus replied,
I see the stings thro' pleasure's snare,
And quick she pass'd each heavenly fair.
With wonder working influence fraught,
Some fair occasion still she caught,
From the wing'd speed of HOURS to take,
Spells that Genius might awake;
With some the path of glory treads,
And there collects his shining deeds;
While some Carmenta's gift supplies,
With song to charm the destinies;

From some she takes and learns to wield,
Virtue's secure protecting shield.

Thus, arm'd to conquer, on she sped,
By Virtue guarded, Judgment led;
She soon the dusky borders found,
Where Genius in soft chains was bound;
And soon her burnish'd shield she shew'd,
Quick thro' the gloom its radiance glow'd;
The gloom receiv'd its influence bright,
And shade dissolv'd in radiant light;
She pure Carmenta's phial draws;
On high the meek petition rose;
And to appease the destinies,
To Genius all its aids supplies;
To softest notes she tun'd her tongue,
And thus she sung Carmenta's song:

Ye nymphs of Pluto's dark domain
    Receive your drowzy God;
With gifts from Phœbus' brilliant train,
    I visit this abode.

If man, by selfish passion sway'd,
    Can pity, hear and spare;
With power and mercy Gods array'd,
    Accept an ardent prayer.

Warm from the heart these words shall rise,
    That must conclude my song;
The Gods will own the sacrifice,
    And their own gifts prolong.

Your gifts shall ever speak your praise,
    Bright attributes of power,
And the rich bounties of your grace
 · To your own glory soar.

Wake Prince, she said, I call thee forth,
Decided is my dubious worth ;
My labours with thy presence crown,
Labours that would be all thy own.

Thy energy must spread the use,
Of this fair phial's limpid juice ;
My labours with thy presence crown,
Labours that would be all thy own.

Fancy would droop without thy aid,
And all its op'ning flowers would fade ;
If fates are sooth'd, to thee belong
The notes that raise the heavenly song.

Let deeds of glory thee inspire ;
Without thee, deeds of fame expire ;

She rose, his presence nature warms,
For him extended all her charms.

He cull'd her gaily op'ning flowers,
And with them dress'd his beauteous bowers;
'Twas he inspir'd the poet's dream,
On northern hills, by Mulla's stream;
Or where the silver waters glide,
Of Thames's deep majestic tide.

When Spencer wrote and Sidney smil'd,
And generous friendship care beguil'd;
Time them on Avon's banks receives,
And amaranthine wreathes he gives;
There fairies frisk beneath the moon,
In darkness witching spells are done.
He touch'd with skill the awful band,
And charmed there the Passions stand.

He tun'd to harmony his tongue,
And thro' the seasons Thomson sung.
Scenes the sublimest thought could find,
He open'd to a Milton's mind;
And oft by contemplation led,
With pensive Grey he sought the shade;
Thro' many an age and many a clime,
These flourish thro' enduring time;

He drew the phial's purest store,
And gave to it a living pow'r;
Thence shone the patriot and the sage,
Examples for the moral page;
Those with its lustre fame supplies,
The rest, perennials of the skies;
Such worth may still Britannia boast,
Tho' she has mourn'd her Howard lost;
Whate'er the favour'd spot of earth
That gave exalted merit birth;
And, as its different lots were cast,
In milder graces it surpass'd;
Or shone with aspect more severe,
Still worth shall kindred worth revere.

Immortal laurels to entwine,
Virtue with Genius must combine;
And Application's active aid
Perform the plan by Judgment laid;
Recorded wonders they can shew,
And means of glorious heights bestow;
They different natures nearly join,
And human make almost divine.

For these to save, thro' wrecks of time belong,
Th' historians faithful page, the muses' heavenly
song.

THOUGHTS

OCCURRING IN THE THEATRE, ON SEEING

Mrs. *SIDDONS*

IN THE CHARACTER OF

BELVIDERA.

QUEEN of expression! on whose potent aid,
Dramatic Genius waits to be display'd,
For tho' presiding o'er that awful cell,*
Where radiant angels or dread demons dwell;
Of thee she asks, to draw them forth to light,
To win the ear, and fascinate the sight;
The drooping heart shall here its griefs resign,
And lose a while its tragic scenes for thine;

The spell which now pervades the weeping hours,
Is Otway's genius, shewn by Siddons' pow'rs ;
Ah ! could he loose the icy bonds of death,
And catch of fame, this hour, a living breath ;
Would he his Belvidera now forego,
Nor think she paid for years of want and woe ;
So shall the bards who hear these matchless strains,
By hope reviv'd forgot their present pains,
Tho' cold neglect now blasts their rising bays,
Otways and Savages of present days ;
Some future Siddons shall redeem their fame,
And stamp IMMORTAL their neglected name;
On thee with fame, deserved fortune wait,
The actor's—different to the poet's fate !

SONNET.

LET not rage to rage opposing,
   Angry passion e'er pursue ;
For kindness a soft charm disclosing,
   Best its fury can subdue.

The sun and wind their power contesting,
   (A tale in Æsop's moral page)
Which the traveller divesting,
   Of his mantle could engage.

The wind his storms then fiercely blowing,
   Saw him his cloak more closely fold ;
But he to the sun warm glowing,
   Yields the prize, and quits his hold.

Where cold suspicions are misleading,
   And with contempt and hatred bind ;
Gentleness for truth best pleading,
   Melts the fetters of the mind.

The frigid blast the shepherd's mourning,
　More firmly bound his streams to see;
Till gentle zephyr mild returning,
　Sets th' imprison'd waters free.

Cold is that heart, of flinty hardness,
　Which mild entreaty cannot move;
But open to the law of kindness,
　Generous bosoms ever prove.

SONNET to CELIA.

No theme the poet more has mourn'd,
   Or faded more his bays;
Than flattery the world has scorn'd,
   For flattery is not praise.

But Celia, while my song shall live,
   Thy merits too shall shine;
Thy worth to praise can sanction give,
   And to preserve be mine.

When what thou wert and they should be,
   The fair in future read,
Them, proud of emulating thee,
   Shall thy example lead.

The beauty whom thy pattern warms,
   No vanity shall stain;
For tho' adorn'd with beauty's charms,
   Celia was never vain.

Her graceful form, her heavenly smile,
 Her cheeks of vermil dye;
Kind nature lavish'd all her spoil,
 My Celia to supply.

The damask rose and lily fair,
 And coral, seas beneath;
The graces gave her winning air,
 The spring her balmy breath.

Mild as fair summer's setting sun,
 Was her benignant eye;
Her voice according hearts has won,
 And discord tun'd to joy.

But nature's gifts improv'd we find,
 Fair Celia can impart;
Charms pointed by her cultur'd mind,
 And virtues of her heart.

TO THE SAME.

NOT every gem a diamond proves,
  Nor every bud a rose;
Nor know we as life onward moves,
  What future days disclose.

Fair Celia when an infant mild,
  Bright hopes her dawn bespoke;
But oft the promise of the child,
  Maturer age has broke.

In Celia numerous virtues shone,
  Each were at generous strife;
Which most adorning we should own,
  In Celia's varied life.

And magnanimity was there,
  And resignation mild;
That firmly could her evils bear,
  Or thro' her tears they smil'd.

And see the generous virtues soar,
 In Celia's happier days;
Soft sympathy to help the poor,
 And the dejected raise.

Hopes which her infant spring had mov'd,
 Meridian days disclose;
And every gem a diamond prov'd,
 And every bud a rose.

SONNET.

EXPERIENCE all silver'd with age,
    Ah! vainly thou visitest me;
Oh! go and the youthful engage,
    To take thee thro' life's troubled sea.

Ah! lead them while blooming and gay,
    To treasure of wisdom a store;
Prosperity may pass away,
    And leave its possessor no more.

Attract them while habits are young,
    To pleasures by virtue refin'd,
And bid them content to prolong,
    In youth firmly ftrengthen the mind.

For kindred, most loving and dear,
    And friendship, that charm of the soul;
Rich cordials life's journey to cheer,
    Have oft bitterness mixt in their bowl.

Nor innocence fame can secure,
  It fades with the blast of a breath;
If virtue our bliss would insure,
  . She points to a state beyond death.

SONNET.

TROUBLED ocean! troubled ocean!
  Thee calmer gales shall sooth to rest;
But what shall smooth that keener motion,
  That rankles in my anxious breast.

Dark clouds the azure skies obscuring,
  Winds waft them, and fair suns appear;
But when my clouded eye is weeping,
  Can aught disperse the bitter tear.

To sable night for Phebus mourning,
  Cynthia lends her placid beam;

M

Oh fay ! what dawn of hope returning,
   On my sorrowing heart shall gleam ?

Thou pliant willow, pliant willow, ·
   That bends and rises from the storm ;
So could I rise from that rude billow,
   Which would o'erwhelm me in the storm.

Oh ! come then heavenly resignation,
   And bear me in the adverse stream ;
Till to celestial bliss I waken,
   From life as from a painful dream.

SONNET.

THE nymphs and the shepherds now mourn,
    That lost is the pride of their grove ;
The cypress o'ershades the sweet rose,
    No more seen is the flow'r which they love.

It's leaves were most spotless and pure,
    Its colours were vivid and gay ;
Its fragrance it lent to the year,
    To the shepherds it brighten'd the day.

The bee would oft make her abode,
    Where sweetness so much did excel ;
Poor insect ! she seeks it in vain,
    And drooping returns to her cell.

New graces each minute display'd,
    No time did its beauty decay :
When, growing the pride of the year,
    'Twas suddenly hurried away.

Such a flower is innocent youth,
    So transient ! so frail in it's bloom ;
So pleasing mild Coridon was,
    As suddenly pass'd to his tomb.

SOLILOQUY.

NATURE ! in all correct, thy hand we trace,
And o'er thy carpet hail a beauteous race;
Each have their station, each their native home,
In adverse soils and climes they find a tomb :
Some in the open lawn, delighted seem
To look with vigour on the sun's full beam :
Whilst some retiring, hide the modest head,
And screen their beauties in the shelt'ring shade :
Some dare the summit of the mountain's brow,
And others humbly seek the vale below :
Some o'er the parched heath minutely spread,
Whilst some, best flourish in the wat'ry mead ;
Deep in the soil others are firmly struck,
Some lightly flaunt upon the sedgy brook,
Others on rocks can independent thrive;
And in rich soil alone can others live.
The gard'ner marks the stations each demand :
Refin'd by cultivation's skilful hand,

Which marks their graces with a clearer line,
And draws each forth more pointedly to shine.

By Providence to different lots assign'd,
A bent so various takes the human mind,
And education marks the native worth,
And boldly calls the leading feature forth,
It fires the hero, or instructs the sage,
To save his country, or reform the age ;
It leads th' ambitious to the public eye,
Or fits the humble for retirement's joy ;
Refines the pleasures of the social scene,
Or teaches industry the art of gain ;
Opens the depth of science unconfin'd,
Researches for the philosophic mind ;
It gives the gay, more graceful to be seen,
Swim on the surface of each trifling scene ;
It can its proper views to fancy give,
And by th' applause of ages bid it live.

Oh happy they ! whose lot thro' life's design'd,
To suit what nature gave, and art refin'd,
Let glory's radiant form the soldier shield,
And courage lead him to the hostile field ;
Give sensibility its social joy,
And for life's trials arm cold apathy.
Fortune and favouring friends may genius see,
All feel the native powers of fancy free ;

Oh ! were the human lot disposed so,
This were a world of joy, scarce mix'd with woe ;
But ah ! full oft we see the tortur'd mind,
Destin'd to trials of ungenial kind,
Where without arms t' oppose, stern foes invade,
And all its native virtues seem to fade ;
The feeling shed not still the tear of joy,
Nor cold disdain meets careless apathy ;
Bright genius roves not still without restraint,
Nor always free his favorite scenes to paint ;
But evils check the wing he lightly spread,
Then warm imagination too must fade.
Reflection in this solitary scene,
Engraves for me the solemn truth within,
As on the moss-grown rock now seated here,
Pain'd memory finds the source of many a tear.

ON FRIENDSHIP.

IF e'er on earth a charm was found,
  To heal our woe, or light up joy ;
The joy is brighten'd, heal'd the wound,
  If friendship's charm we can employ.

Love is a transient flame at best,
  As vivid lightnings glaring fly ;
And must with friendship quickly rest,
  Or soon with cold indifference die.

Its root is deep, its growth is slow,
  Its native soil the generous heart ;
And they can only friendship know,
  Who sympathy to all impart.

'Tis not to glitt'ring wealth confin'd,
  Or blooming beauty's smiling morn ;

It clings to beauties of the mind,
  And virtues that the heart adorn.

So cherish'd, it may only stand
  A numerous host of treacherous foes,
That rise a mean and hostile band,
  Their baneful influence to oppose.

Suspicion knows but to disgust,
  With clouded brow and squinting eye;
And cold reserve and mean distrust,
  Their base and chilling arts employ.

Friendship! sublimest good on earth:
  It claims our tender constant care;
But if such foes oppose its worth,
  No wonder it is seen so rare.

THOUGHTS

OCCASIONED BY THE DEATH OF

AN AMIABLE YOUTH,

WHILE HIS FRIENDS WERE MET TO CELEBRATE HIS BIRTH-DAY.

———————

A LOVELY plant a garden grac'd,
   'Twas call'd the village pride ;
For poor seem'd many a goodly flow'r,
   While blowing by its side.

With festive mirth and heart-felt joy,
   The village swains resort,
And yearly, as it fresher blew,
   They held a rural sport.

The Sun had eighteen circles run,
　　It blew more bright and fair ;
They met, admir'd the Former's skill,
　　And pray'd his future care.

Gracious he stoop'd to view his work,
　　View'd it with pitying eyes ;
To save it from the storms, he said,
　　Transplant it to the skies.

SONG.

HAPPY ! happy ! happy Woman !
    Thou art nature's darling care ;
She only gave his strength to man,
    To be the guardian of the fair.

As in the Anana we can trace
    Each delicious fruit combin'd,
And in the diamond's varied blaze,
    The hue of every gem we find.

So nature's charms collected are
    In sweet woman's lovely frame,
Whate'er is charming, fine, or rare,
    In woman can be seen the same.

Mistaking man, himself may check,
    He happy woman still approves ;

Whene'er it pleases her to speak,
　'Tis sweet to him, as vocal groves.

Man may be doom'd to wander far,
　Happy woman needs not roam;
The fruits of peace, and spoils of war,
　He brings to her, delighted, home.

Study nor labour man withstands;
　Neither can fair woman need,
She must not tire her lily hands,
　Or dim her shining eyes to read.

That women food and raiment share,
　Man his vigour spends and prime;
Whilst she thinks what to eat and wear,
　And how to spend her happy time.

She must not soil her dainty foot,
　While man the bitter storm must know;
He bears her cheerfully about,
　Where'er it is her mind to go.

A rout, a play, a masquerade,
　Is happy woman's pleasant sphere;
Man ever racks his careful head,
　For something new her heart to cheer.

Man's stubborn heart grief deeply shares,
  If bitter moisture fills his eye;
If nature gave to woman tears,
  She only meant them tears of joy.

That age decays is nature's doom:
  But art can mysteries unfold;
Olympian dew, Circassian bloom;
  And happy woman ne'er is old.

Since woman is so blest on earth,
  Be man alone the prey of death;
Some antidote let art bring forth,
  And woman keep her fragrant breath.

THE QUESTION.

MAY those who dress each future year,
  With fairy scenes of promis'd joy,
Let fame and glitt'ring fortune hear,
  And feel the magic they employ.

While I with humble hopes and pow'rs,
  Would seek an unaspiring theme,
That points me out no golden hours,
  Nor oft inspires the poet's dream.

Say what is that, where fully given
  Nought else its owner can possess ?
But never shall it be in heaven,
  And none its name shall ever bless.

Yet is it not despis'd of heaven,
  Which ought its mis'ry still to cheer,

For to the son of God 'twas given
   And was his constant portion here.

It faints beneath the torrid sun,
   And shivers in the northern snows;
And should it weary labour shun,
   Must soon, alas! in death repose.

Beneath the scourge, and unredrest,
   It sinks into the grave it delves;
But Britons* though of this possest,
   Yet ever may possess themselves

Indifference dwells for ever near,
   All charms it vainly would apply;
Its wisdom seldom gains the ear,
   . Nor oft its beauty wins the eye.

If in the shiftings of the scene,
   O POVERTY! I thee should know,
'Twill surely soothe some pang within,
   That I have felt for others woe.

Ye poor, yet brethren! fellow clay!
   And in our common nature bound,

---

* Slavery cannot breathe in England.

               MANSFIELD.

Oh! may the rich attention pay,
   Where'er your simple history's found.

Oh! be they to your virtues kind,
   Your woes their pity ever gain,
Your errors, may their candour find,
   Rememb'ring you, as they, are men.

SONNET.

FORSAKE the sparkling eye of joy,
   On downy wing, oh! balmy sleep;
Swift all thy gentle power employ,
   To close the eyes that weep.

Confin'd within their ebon cell,
   All thy terrific visions stay;
Wide, where thy dreams of pleasure dwell,
   The ivory gates display.

The sickening heart thy powers release,
   From every felt, or threaten'd harm;

Let former days return to bless,
   And fond illusions charm.

Whate'er of dear departed good,
   The pensive mourner can deplore;
Thou may'st, in paths with pleasure strew'd,
   Kindly again restore.

There—bliss of youth ! th' approving friend,
   And health, and dear parental love;
Joys, which all earthly joys transcend,
   With the freed spirit rove.

Oh sleep ! display thy visions fair,
   Where grief has sown its thorns within;
Till death, dissolving mortal care,
   Shall realize the scene.

N

LINES

*Occasioned by my putting a Bee out of my Window
one cold Morning in February, at the request of
a Child.*

———

AH beauteous stranger ! here too soon,
  For pity came too late ;
Granted to fear a coward boon,
  And thee resign'd to fate.

The deed which stopp'd thy honied breath,
  Convey'd a sting to me ;
Grieving the fatal gift was death,
  Which I meant liberty.

Nature thy golden plumage drest,
  And tun'd thy simple note ;

But yet a niggard of her feast,
  My erring hand forgot.

No vernal robe, or summer sweet,
  Blossoms or plant display ;
A herald of the spring to greet,
  Nor sunbeam cheer'd thy way.

Black Eurus chill'd thy infant wing,
  Dread wastes affright thine eye ;
Opening the vocal choir of spring,
  Stern winter bid thee die.

Ah ! what avails a bounteous store,
  Or what a heart to give ;
When the important minute's o'er,
  That sufferers might receive ?

A STRAYED CHILD.

A STEM blown from its parent tree,
　　I planted in my humble bower;
Sure it may grow to shelter me,
　　From scorching sun and dripping shower.

Stay Madelina, child of woe,
　　Thy little feet no more shall roam,
I said, and fast as tears could flow,
　　Mine fell, and pity took thee home.

The dewy ground was then thy bed,
　　Its canopy, the arch of Heaven;
On a cold stone reclin'd thy head,
　　Thy mouldy scraps were hardly given.

Ill suited was thy motley dress,
　Refuse of infancy and age;
So sorted, as to shew distress,
　Not screen thee from the tempest's rage.

But on thy face yet health could glow,
　There unreflecting smiles were seen:
For transient joy so temper'd woe,
　To cheer thy little heart within.

By want torn from thy parent tree,
　Here hapless Madelina come;
My little shall be shar'd with thee,
　I'll be thy parent—here's thy home.

WILLIAM AND ELLEN.

WHERE Nature gives exterior grace,
  Oh might she inward worth impart!
Then safely charm'd the beauteous face;
  For form'd to bless the virtuous heart.

Young William houses had, and land,
  And shining gold, a plenteous store;
But he than house, or fertile land,
  Or shining gold, lov'd Ellen more.

Where Ellen was, love would be there,
  And his seducing arts employ;
He waved the ringlets in her hair,
  And shone in her resplendent eye.

Had other graces been allied,
  Mingling her many charms among,

Tho' William's suit had been denied,
   He had not died of grief and wrong.

Tho' conquest 'twas her pride to gain,
   Small her desert true love to have;
She frown'd on worth with cold disdain,
   And triumph'd in the pain she gave.

But patient William's gentle love,
   Tried every winning art to please;
And still his constancy would prove,
   And apt occasions ever seize.

If Ellen were at fair or wake,
   At wake or fair was William too;
Still some impression hop'd to make,
   And lovely Ellen's heart subdue.

He treated her with cakes most rare,
   Rich wine, to please the nicest taste,
Gay ribbons to adorn her hair,
   And shining girdles for her waist.

At eve, when village maids return'd,
   And met around her cottage door,
Displaying gifts their conquests earn'd,
   Ellen's exceeded far their store.

But ah! those gifts with scorn were ta'en,
   Her hand to him she could refuse ;
Nor join the dance with such a swain
   As any other maid would choose.

But mighty Love has often sworn
   To punish those who scorn his pow'r ;
The pain they gave he will return,
   And meet them in a fatal hour.

She, who would still at William sneer,
   Could Edward's little merit raise ;
To him incline a listening ear,
   And brighten at his scanty praise.

Ah Ellen ! wert thou rich as fair,
   The churlish Edward careless cried,
Thy riches I should like to share,
   And take thee, Ellen, for my bride.

If riches thou would'st have with me,
   And rich, I soon should be thy bride ;
My riches thou shalt quickly see,
   The cruel Ellen straight replied.

On William now her shining eye,
   Beam'd, soften'd of her wonted scorn ;

She feign'd to meet the youth with joy,
  Who late had deem'd himself forlorn.

How rais'd was William's drooping heart,
  All banish'd his desponding fears ;
To him her smiles of hours impart,
  Joy that o'erpaid the scorn of years.

She met him at the wake or fair,
  And with him in the dance would join ;
Nor seem'd she to have other care,
  Nor wish to other swain to shine.

My charming Ellen what delays,
  He said, that we join willing hands ;
What now the happy minute stays,
  Till we unite in wedlock's bands ?

Then Ellen forc'd a mimic sigh,
  On him reclin'd her blushing face ;
Ah ! well if his too partial eye,
  Had mark'd it not the blush of grace.

Can faithful William yet forgive
  One boon that maiden pride demands ?
Granted, it shall no more survive ;
  And straight, she said, we'll join our hands.

Whate'er my Ellen shall demand,
    The rich reward, he cried, outweighs ;
Where she bestows her charming hand,
    What favor can have equal praise.

Name thy request my lovely maid,
    And make me happy to bestow ;
Some noble tribute should be paid,
    William's unbounded love to show.

You, she return'd, I mean to wed ;
    But, highly tho' you rate my charms,
Of William it shall ne'er be said,
    He took a beggar to his arms.

Then bring to me a shining dower ;
    'Tis but the whim and pride of youth ;
One effort of expiring power,
    To try thy matchless love and truth.

Then bring me here thy shining gold ;
    The writings of thy fertile land ;
And of thy buildings fair and bold :
    To be return'd with my true hand.

For with the morrow's risen sun,
    When thou hast me so nobly dower'd,

All shall to thee be truly done,
  Which thou hast generously empower'd.

For when our guests, sat round our board,
  Are viewing me, a beauteous bride,
I'll spread thy gold, a shining hoard,
  And say, to love I gold confide.

And there I'll spread thy writings fair,
  And say, my William take my land;
I give thee too my houses rare;
  For with myself my all command.

Then all our guests, with high applause,
  Shall say, Fair Ellen, nobly done;
A just reward crowns William's cause;
  For he a generous maid has won.

And be it so, true William cried;
  Soon shalt thou have the generous power,
A splendid fortune to confide,
  And, with thyself, bestow a dower.

To her he counted out his gold;
  To her he made his fertile land;
All his fair houses strong and bold:
  To be return'd with her true hand.

And now, he said, to-morrow's sun,
　　Shall not behold a happier swain;
That charming maid shall then be won,
　　For whom I fear'd to sigh in vain.

William, she said, remember then,
　　That holy church shall make us one;
To-morrow, at the hour of ten,
　　There meet the maid thou well hast won.

But never rose the morrow's sun,
　　On a more false or perjur'd maid;
A maid was surely ne'er so won,
　　Or lover with such wrong repaid.

Nor was there at the hour of ten,
　　A youth so overwhelm'd with woe;
To holy church went William then;
　　And learnt what rent his heart to know.

At nine, false Ellen there had been,
　　And Edward met to give her hand;
So wrong'd, what youth was ever seen,
　　Of love, of gold, of house and land!

William, a wretched wanderer goes,
　　And begs in bitterness each meal;

That Ellen wrought his wrongs and woes,
 Doubles the pangs he's doom'd to feel.

Long years he wander'd thus in woe,
 Ere death would bring its kind relief;
Or wretched William was laid low,
 By want, and slow consuming grief.

Oft marriage may a veil remove,
 Which passion waits not to unfold :
Ellen soon found that Edward's love,
 Was but the love of William's gold.

Then conscience rent her bleeding heart,
 For wrong to generous William wrought ;
And to return some little part,
 She Edward tenderly besought.

Oh ! of his own to William give,
 She said, and soothe my heart with peace ;
Oh ! grant him but the means to live,
 My tongue to bless thee shall not cease.

Unequal as the sunny beam,
 The hard unfeeling rock to melt,
Did Ellen's words on Edward seem ;
 His flinty heart as little felt.

Yet ever thro' each mournful year,
  To Edward she made fruitless prayer,
That he would to be just appear,
  And hapless William something spare.

A wreck of sorrow, all but trace
  Where dazzling charms were lov'd so well ;
But deadlier paleness spread her face,
  When hollow sounded William's bell.

At night when all were gone to rest,
  But she whose sorrow spared no room,
Dead William, in his grave-clothes drest,
  To Ellen came, or seem'd to come.

Cold was the hand which touch'd her thrice ;
  And pale the face she seem'd to see ;
And hollow was the trembling voice,
  Which said, My Ellen come to me.

Not thy disdain my love could daunt ;
  For years of scorn I well lov'd thee ;
Thro' years of wrong, and years of want ;
  And now, my Ellen, come to me.

Oh William ! thou art pale and cold,
  She said ; and murder'd art by me ;

I cannot give thee back thy gold;
　But, William, I will go with thee.

Thrice then he kiss'd her trembling hand;
　And thrice, with clay-cold lips, her cheek;
Then forth he drew a silken band,
　And bound it round her lily neck.

Upon her pillow, sunk her head;
　She spoke no word, she heav'd no sigh;
She stretch'd herself upon her bed;
　And so did hapless Ellen die.

SONNET.

———

THE wise, thro' time, have join'd to say
   That bliss on earthly ground,
To mix, and deep, with some allay,
   Will soon or late be found.

Yet, once I strove by fancy's aid
   To dress, and call it mine;
A joy that nothing here could shade,
   It seem'd so near divine.

I every generous virtue sought;
   And plac'd them in a heart
With noble feelings finely fraught,
   Devoid of pride or art.

I form'd a head, few such have been,
   No gaudy sepulchre;
Which, if the poor contents were shewn,
   But few would wish it near.

Rich treasures there, in memory's store,
  Bid Taste and Learning place;
With Judgment to collect still more,
  And brilliant Wit to grace.

These with a pleasing form I crown'd,
  Sure tis offence to no man;
My sex I own I wish'd renown'd,
  And call'd my charm a woman.

But blessings dress'd by fancy's light,
  I fear'd must fleet away;
Till Clara shone upon my sight,
  And bid my vision stay.

Oh Clara! such a charm as thee,
  But one way finds to grieve me;
And that, my Clara, cannot be,
  That thou shouldst wish to leave me.

O

SONG.

Dear Clara, pray pass this small trouble,
   And with us contentedly dwell;
When the creature within is so noble,
   How little we think of its cell.

The soul, be it e'er so refin'd,
   Must live in a cottage of clay;
And the Lord of the world was consign'd
   To lie in a manger on hay.

No place all our wishes supplies,
   Then the best we can offer pray take;
For Fortune is ever so wise,
   Not to venture us all at a stake.

Then Clara resign to our love,
   This little of what you may want;
And when Fortune such merit shall prove,
   Your favorite wish she may grant.

SONG.

THIS is a world of right and wrong;
   A world of pleasure and of pain;
A world to which rich gifts belong,
   That some can never gain.

A world, where health and wealth enjoy,
   And sickness clouds the brow;
Some active spirits can employ,
   And some are humbled low.

Many with numerous friends are seen,
   By tender cares carest;
Whilst others desolate remain,
   As in a dreary waste.

It is a world of ease and care,
   A world of joy and woe;
And rosy youth runs smiling there,
   And sorrowing age treads slow.

It is not Nature's joy or woe,
   Makes all the medley here ;
The moral world the same can shew ;
   They mix'd, alike appear.

No perfect conquest here below,
   Has vice or virtue made ;
Thro' vice some gleams of virtue glow,
   And virtue takes a shade.

Then in this world of joy and woe,
   This world of good and ill,
The will of him who made it so,
   Oh ! study to fulfil.

To many wants, you who abound !
   Dispense your blessing's store :
For scarce a grief or want is found,
   Where none a balm may pour.

Give ignorance instruction due ;
   Be vice example shewn ;
And let us faults with pity view,
   As conscious of our own.

SONNET.

WHEN first you sought my rural cot,
　　And found my friendship there ;
Daphne, contented with your lot,
　　You shar'd my simple fare.

I chill'd you not with cold reserve,
　　Nor wore a haughty frown ;
Tho' what your merit might deserve,
　　Was yet to me unknown.

A cheerful welcome to impart,
　　I spread my little stores ;
And oft I rais'd your drooping heart,
　　With hopes of happier hours.

To you my friendship lent its aid,
　　And call'd its vigour forth ;
For prosp'rous scenes it wish'd display'd,
　　To unassuming worth.

It was not fed by airy dreams,
  Nor hop'd for high return;
Nor could it fear the hard extremes,
  Of hate and haughty scorn.

———————

SONNET.

———

A TENDER care, that's ever near,
  A friend most true and kind;
In faithful Jenny shall endear,
  While human ties can bind.

Her gentle smile improves my joy,
  Her tears can sooth my grief;
She reads the language of my eye,
  And brings my heart relief.

Then if I lack a golden store,
  A treasure I possess;
For Jenny makes my pleasures more,
  And all my sorrows less.

But should a brighter fortune come,
  There Jenny should appear;
For she would share my saddest doom,
  And try that doom to cheer.

Oh may her comfort still be nigh,
  To sooth my life and death!
Oh may she close my dying eye,
  And watch my parting breath!

SONG.

———

No constancy here dwells,
   Upon our earthly ground :
But like the merry bells,
   All have their changes round.

To the poor infants cries,
   Succeeds gay youthful bloom ;
Then strength and wisdom rise,
   Till second childhood come.
       No constancy, &c.

And riches make them wings,
   And take themselves away ;
Then friendship from you flings,
   Nor will a moment stay.
       No constancy, &c.

And health that gilds our days,
   May pallid sickness shade :

And while our frame decays,
  Our pleasures too must fade.
    No constancy, &c.

Then should the young sustain,
  And lend their strength to age;
That they may comfort gain,
  In life's concluding stage.
    No constancy, &c.

Tho' fickle Fortune frown,
  Let friends be true and kind ;
Lest wealth from them be flown,
  And they no friendship find.

    For constancy here never dwells,
      Upon our earthly ground :
    But like the merry bells,
      All have their changes round.

ODE TO HEALTH.

DAUGHTER of temperance and peace,
  Auspicious Health appear !
Thee aromatic crowns shall grace,
  Rich odours of the year.
To form thy robe's resplendent glow,
Their emblems light and hope bestow,
  Thy hands with treasures pure, *
(Whilst ever round thy hallow'd shrine,
Life's salutary figures twine,)
  In blessing can secure.

---

* Health is represented holding a golden globe. She is placed near an
altar, around which a serpent is entwined, which is an attribute of health,
being the least liable to malady of any reptile.

                              See Richardson's Iconolog.

For thee, each power, each gift must hope,
   Without thy sanction vain ;
Depress'd and fetter'd, these must droop,
   And joyless those remain.
For ah ! within a languid frame,
Enjoyment is an empty name,
   And fond pursuits subside.
Ye days and scenes, once fair to view!
A sympathetic languor too,
   O'ershades your summer's pride.

Dealing its wish to every sense,
   Riches their stores unfold ;
Vainly are pleasures hop'd from thence,
   If health withdraws from gold.
By her enrich'd, content in mind,
Observe the beggar now reclin'd
   In yonder fertile vale ;
Pleasant he eats his homely meal,
Drinks the pure water from the rill,
   And cons his plaufive tale.

A SICK FRIEND.

THO' from the feeling heart be kindred torn,
And early friends, by chance or change, it mourn;
While it inhabits in this middle sphere,
Where good and ill for ever mix'd appear.
Not for itself, alone, it can survive ;
Supporting and supported it would live ;
Feel its best joys in soothing others woes,
And would its own in some kind breast repose ;
Native affections still around it play,
And fondly bind it to its fellow-clay.
Best bliss of life, if joy they can diffuse,
And that seems dearest which we fear to lose.

Ah! be no parting tye more mourn'd by me,
Nor I, Eliza, doom'd to grieve.for thee.
May health return, and still thy friendship bless;
And none who love me, leave me in my race.
Denied by distance to my anxious sight,
I cannot cheer thy day, and watch thy night.
Denied the tender cares, by friendship taught,
I cannot give the salutary draught:
And anxious hopes, and fears, and prayers are mine,
Till cheerful days, and health again be thine.

THOUGHTS

BEFORE THE

INTERMENT OF A FRIEND.

FAREWEL! farewel! and art thou gone !
   And canst thou cheer my sight no more !
Ah ! long alas shall I bemoan,
   What earth can ne'er restore.

That eye, a feeling heart disclos'd,
   And was my fond delight to see ;
But now it is for ever clos'd,
   Nor more shall beam on me.

The gentle accents of that tongue,
   The sound of that beloved voice,
Where oft my pleas'd attention hung,
   No more can me rejoice.

That heart, once open to my view,
   No generous aim can now complete ;
That heart, so tender and so true,
   Alas ! has ceas'd to beat.

That head, where bright ideas play'd,
   Unus'd from studious thought to shrink ;
No more its charms to me shall spread,
   It ceases now to think.

No circulating blood to warm,
   But pale and lifeless seen,
Is that once animated form,
   That spoke a soul within.

That form so dear, now lifeless clay,
   We mingle with the dead ;
To joys beyond what we can say,
   Be its lov'd spirit fled.

UPON FINDING

THE INSCRIPTION

ON MY

MOTHER's MONUMENT

DEFACED.

———————

THESE tender records of thy worth are gone ;
From them thy merit shall no more be known.
But cease my tears, thy dust regrets it not,
Forgetting all, as all shall be forgot ;
And he alas ! whose power no more could give,
Than by this marble wish thy name to live ;
Here often caused my thoughtless youth to come,
And learn a lovely pattern from thy tomb ;
He, now with thee, is here in silence laid,
Unconscious of the wrecks which Time has made.

Let Time proceed to that important hour,
When its last victory shall conclude its power.
Then, tho' a mouldering stone no more conveys,
The doubtful plaudit of a human praise;
Tho' Taste and Learning here have not avail'd;
And e'en the records that they were have fail'd;
If pure Devotion, and if steady Truth,
Were unremitted from thy early youth;
Then take thy mansion in yon upper skies:
The God of truth accepts the sacrifice.
If mindful to increase thy mental stores,
Thou diligently caught the flying hours;
As then no stranger to the work of Heaven,
With ampler powers shall ampler means be given.
If with the utmost that thou couldst attain,
Of shining merits thou wert never vain;
Tho' in thy prime cut off from earthly praise,
Wisdom has been to thee as length of days.
If here th'allotted duties of thy sphere,
Thou deem'd thy fairest praise, and dearest care;
As in thy station thus thou fitly mov'd,
Thou shalt arise accepted and approv'd:
Tho' lost to earth, in Heaven thou shalt be found,
And glories visible shall thee surround.

P

HYMNS.

ATTENDANCE

UPON

RELIGIOUS INSTITUTIONS.

I'LL bless Jehovah's glorious name,
Whose goodness heaven and earth proclaim,
 With every morning's light;
And at the close of ev'ry day,
To him my cheerful homage pay,
 Who guards me thro' the night.

Then in his churches to appear,
And pay my humble worship there,
 Shall be my sweet employ;
The day that saw my Saviour rise,
Shall dawn on my delighted eyes,
 With every sacred joy.

With grateful sorrow in my breast,
I'll celebrate the dying feast,
    Of my departing Lord;
And while his perfect love I view,
His bright example I'll pursue,
    And meditate his word.

FOR

EASTER SUNDAY.

———

HAIL! this morn's auspicious light,
That rose upon the gloom of night:
Mortals! your tongues should never cease
To hail the glorious Prince of Peace.

Sons of men, he dwelt with you,
The perfect rule of life he drew:
See your Saviour's matchless love,
For you, severest sorrows prove.

The friend of man, he yields his breath,
Despis'd in life, revil'd in death;
But grief and pain, and death he bore,
To soften their tyrannic pow'r.

Arise and shine, our light is come,
He breaks the prison of the tomb :
Celestial Hero ! wide display,
The banners of eternal day.

We'll rest our hopes upon his word,
And wait the coming of our Lord ;
The power of death no more we'll dread,
For Christ is risen from the dead.

Hail ! this morn's auspicious light,
That rose upon the gloom of night ;
Mortals, your tongues should never cease,
To hail the glorious Prince of Peace.

HYMN

Sung at a Charity Sermon, in Lancaster, on the 22d of January, 1797, for the Blind Asylum, Liverpool.

———

SUMMON'D before Jehovah's throne,
    Conscience would shrink with fear ;
If Heaven had not its mercy shewn,
    And sent a Saviour here.

One great command that Saviour gave,
    Whose life redeem'd from sin ;
That tender mercies, call'd to save,
    Should thro' our lives be seen.

To aid, to sooth the poor distrest,
    The righteous must rejoice :
And every Christian's feeling breast,
    Be tun'd to pity's voice.

While we behold the grateful light,
 Can read th' instructive page;
May those debarr'd the bliss of sight,
 All tenderness engage.

God's wond'rous works they cannot trace,
 In Nature's beauteous train;
For veil'd to them her lovely face,
 Her seasons change in vain.

To them descends no beam of light;
 No suns have splendid shone;
And but the changing day and night,
 By rest or labour known.

The poor and blind must claim your care;
 Ye rich! tis yours to bless;
In pity needless wants oh spare!
 And give to their distress.

Oh pour instructions on their mind!
 Oh! cheer their dark abode!
And to their every want be kind;
 Tis in the heavenly road

NEW YEAR's DAY.

AGAIN time's ever fleeting hand
  Points to the finish'd year ;
It's moments with past ages stand,
  Nor more for me appear,

Say has improvement mark'd your flight,
  Seasons in mercy given ?
Does the recording angel write
  His testimony, heaven ?

For tho' from me for ever flown,
  Unchang'd yon awful mount ;
And angels smile, or fiends you frown
  Upon my last account.

Then as the opening dawn I hail,
   Of time to me renew'd ;
Be what I do and where I fail,
   Impartially review'd.

And while th' important moments pass,
   And time again revolves ;
Spirit of power and heavenly grace,
   Assist my weak resolve.

From each imperfect virtuous part,
   Then purer good shall spring ;
From errors past, a contrite heart,
   Sainted repentance bring.

A HYMN IN SICKNESS:

THIS mortal life may soon be over,
   Adieu ! adieu to all I know !
The dust may soon my body cover,
   But whither shall my spirit go ?

Ere I hope pardon thro' his blood.
   Or can my Saviour's ransom claim ;
Or dare aspire to Heaven's abode,
   Tell me conscience what I am ?

By him, the Universal Lord,
   Have I sought to be approv'd ?
Him have I humbly still ador'd,
   And gratefully my Maker lov'd ?

Are thy commands, O God of truth,
   Still my pleasure to obey ?
Have they temper'd well my youth,
   And are they guards to guide my way ?

And do I shew my love to thee,
   Whom my eyes have never seen ;
By love to those who are like me,
   Subject to sorrow and to sin ?

As all my errors I've revolv'd,
   Do I repent as I survey ?
Them have I faithfully resolv'd,
   To leave thro' every future day.

FOR SUNDAY.

THIS is that day of sacred rest,
   For holy meditation chose ;.
Then soar my thoughts among the blest,
   And let my mortal cares repose.

The joys above are painted here,
   By figures which the sense receives ;
But how their glories shall appear,
   We know no human heart conceives.

The sacred leisure of this day,
   · Let me improve for God and heaven ;
To bliss that I secure my way,
   To me on earth were Sabbaths given.

Now be my virtues all renew'd
   And heavenly consolation speak ;
Holy resolves be well pursued,
   And guard the duties of the week.

HYMN FOR SUNDAY.

TWO great events this blessed day
    To celebrate was set apart;
While each, with wonder, we survey,
    May gratitude impress the heart.

This day creation's birth be hail'd,
    And may our thoughts ascend on high;
Let him who over death prevail'd,
    Our thankful praises too employ.

God's powerful word creation fram'd,
    Six days, and all complete it stood;
The seventh a day of rest he nam'd,
    And he beheld, and all was good.

This day be worldly cares subdu'd,
    Holy improvement may we seek;
While still with strict survey review'd,
    We trace the actions of the week.

Of duties still be this a part ;
  This day the saving work pursue ;
'Twill humble every haughty heart ;
  For pride, self-knowledge never knew.

This day we hear the blessed word
  Which bids our hearts no more despond ;
We celebrate our risen Lord,
  Who seal'd for us a heavenly bond.

                                4.

OMNIPRESENCE OF GOD.

———————

IF I to God my ways approve,
  How can my spirit yield to fear;
Should earthly comforts all remove,
  My heavenly friend is ever near.

He's with me thro' the busy day,
  And thro' the silence of the night;
Attends me in my public way,
  And when retir'd I meet his sight.

If tempters try my soul to win,
  He sees my struggle, and the snare;
And if I, yielding, dare to sin,
  The God whom I offend is there.

If grief should in my heart prevail,
   And every aid should me forsake ;
Sleep to my weary eye should fail,
   And food in bitterness I take :

Tho' I in overwhelming fears,
   To earthly friends in vain apply ;
Check'd be my sighs, restrained my tears,
   The God who can protect is nigh.

If earth's to me a world of joy,
   And he who bless'd me is forgot ;
The power is by who can destroy,
   The giver, whom I have not sought.

When first I drew my vital breath,
   I was my Maker's present care ;
And when my heart expires in death,
   God, my supporter, will be there.

HIS IMMENSITY.

NOT heaven alone is thine abode,
  Maker and Lord of all ;
For thou, the ever present God,
  Pervadest thro' the whole.

The gentle zephyr speaks thy love ;
  Thunders and storms thy power :
Thou shin'st in suns, and stars above ;
  And here in every flower.

Not present more where man is plac'd,
  In groves and flowery meads :
Than rocks and sea and barren waste,
  And where no footstep treads.

Q

Yet not to earth and those it own,
　Thou, Lord, can'st be confin'd;
Thro' thy creation equal known,
　Acknowledg'd, present, kind.

Thro' all diffus'd, o'er all enthron'd,
　Immense is thine abode;
Beyond what countless worlds can bound,
　Thro' all th'existing God.

OMNISCIENCE.

PURE Source ! existing every where;
  From whom life flows, an endless stream;
Bright knowledge ! unsuspended, clear !
  With all, and over all, supreme.

Plain to thy comprehensive view,
  Thy whole creation stands display'd ;
No thought the human heart e'er knew,
  But he who made the heart survey'd.

Tho' human powers may feel decay,
  And memory's records be erased ;
God's knowledge ever can survey,
  What his minute research has traced.

And with the past and present seen,
  To him is every future age,

Before him as they now had been,
　Still busy on life's active stage.

His plans are undisturb'd and clear,
　His wise designs shall still prevail,
For he, great God, is every where ;
　Nor can his knowledge ever fail.

Not bound to temples made with hands,
　Each heart its altar can prepare :
The universe his temple stands ;
　And universal rise the prayer.

Eternal judge, from whose survey,
　No colouring, no art can screen ;
To thee display'd, as light in day,
　Hypocrisy is ever seen.

Then may I pray, and may I fear,
　Nor circumspection e'er depart ;
But let me think how I appear,
　To God, the searcher of the heart.

If he's my comfort and support,
　The world may slander or despise ;
I'll patient bear each false report,
　If clear'd to his allseeing eyes.

For what I only can propose,
    He'll honour and reward impart :
He all its generous purpose knows,
    He knows the meaning of my heart.

If grief for sins my spirit feel,
    And sinks abash'd into despair,
He separates the good from ill,
    And marks my leading character.

WISDOM.

INFINITE Wisdom ! nature's source
    Whate'er thy hand has wrought,
Each in its rank pursues its course,
    By thee divinely taught.

Thy heavens in dazzling beauty shine,
    And silent order move ;
And still fulfilling thy design,
    Their Maker's wisdom prove.

Nor needs the eye of man to soar
    Beyond his own abode ;
Whate'er its search can there explore,
    Proclaims alike a God.

Earth fill'd with life, with beauty dress'd,
    Thy wisdom's work and care ;
Whilst Man, its lord, high o'er the rest,
    Appears a wonder there.

His curious frame, more curious mind,
  His heart, with feeling fraught;
By heavenly wisdom were design'd,
  And wonderfully wrought.

God not to lower being gave,
  Reason, man's suited guide;
But order'd instinct there to save,
  Where reason was denied.

Upon thy wisdom, mighty lord,
  Shall thy creation rest;
It safe protection can afford,
  And still contrives the best.

Its means are sure, its end is right,
  In each unerring plan;
Thro' all thy works it beams its light,
  Upon the mind of man.

Oh may these thoughts possess my mind,
  Inspire my hope and trust;
Since whatsoever God designs,
  Is wisest, best, most just.

GOODNESS of GOD.

———

IMMENSE ! eternal, mighty Lord !
   Dreadful thou wouldst appear ;
Thy power with trembling awe ador'd,
   If justice were severe.

But animated goodness beams
   On our transported view ;
Mild justice fills our grateful themes
   With love and wonder too.

Not that thro' ages still the same,
   Thy being takes its course ;
Not that thy hand thro' nature's frame,
   Impels with equal force :

Not that thro' worlds and boundless space,
    Is thine immense domain ;
Not that thy knowledge all can trace,
    And wisdom all ordain :

But that thy goodness shall endure,
    Long as thyself shalt last ;
That with thy power it rests secure,
    Wide as thy reign is placed.

Omniscient to discern the best,
    The fittest means to choose ;
Of wisdom to contrive the best,
    And boundless good diffuse.

With distant awe we view thy power ;
    Thy wisdom we admire ;
But 'tis the goodness we adore,
    That love and hope inspire !

POWER AND PROVIDENCE.

THE God to whom at one survey
   His works are still display'd,
And each event observes his sway,
   Thro' all which he has made ;

Can order from disorder bring,
   Thro' all this varied scene ;
Can regulate each secret spring,
   That moves the vast machine.

Upheld by his supporting arm,
   Empires can fear no foe ;
His frown strikes nations with alarm ;
   They fall if he withdraw.

And nought so little, or so great,
   But his protection share ;
And he who rules o'er empire's fate,
   Makes man alike his care.

'Tis he relieves the wants we feel,
   To human power denied ;
He guards us from impending ill,
   Which we could ne'er avoid.

The joys we prize would quickly blast,
   Denied his sov'reign aid ;
And all our prudence could forecast,
   Would disappointment shade.

MERCY.

'Tis on thy mercy, gracious Lord,
'Tis on the promise of thy word,
That we thy creatures dare depend,
And call thee father, heavenly friend!

O God our Maker hear our prayer,
Guard us from every sinful snare:
Thee may we trust, in thee rejoice,
And nothing hate or fear but vice.

Thy pity let our errors move;
And oh! our penitence approve:
Thou who mad'st us, knows how frail,
And thy compassions never fail.

Thou on repentance wilt forgive,
And biddest us return and live;
Return and every sin abjure;
And let the heart and life be pure.

Oh God of mercy ! God of love !
If from thy paths we ever rove,
Let us not long in misery droop,
Nor lose our sight of heavenly hope.

If from thy presence wander'd far,
Let not the Gates of mercy bar ;
But oh repentant may we be,
Tho' it be horror, agony !

RESIGNATION.

I HAVE a home, it is not here;
    Then here would anxious cares be wrong;
For I must dwell for ever there ;
    And here I must not tarry long.

I would but take a traveller's care,
    For what I meet, in this my road ;
If coarse or fine should be my fare,
    My way with thorns or roses strew'd.

If I my lov'd companions lose,
    Let me not loiter in my way ;
Nor study here what I would choose ;
    As if my journey were my stay.

For when I bid this earth farewell,
    And at my home my spirit lands,
I shall find friends will never fail,
    And have a house that ever stands.

MORNING HYMN.

OH thou restorer of my frame!
  I thank thy love, I bless thy name,
For peace and safety thro' this night,
  For health, and for returning light.

Oh! may I rise prepared to meet,
  What thou for me shall think most fit;
Prepared my duties to pursue,
  In all my hand can find to do.

To call on thee my gracious lord,
  To read and to observe thy word
To rule my house with pious care,
  And strive that love and peace be there.

Each portion of my time to fill
   Neglect no good, and do no ill ;
To guard my heart, restrain my tongue,
   And patiently to suffer wrong.

That when again the day shall close,
   My conscience break not my repose ;
But I may view the day when past,
   Well pleas'd, tho' it should be my last.

MORNING HYMN.

AGAIN I wake, Almighty Lord,
　　Collect my thoughts, and call on thee;
Who hast my thinking powers restor'd,
　· And in thy mercy guarded me.

To thought and action I revive,
　　And leave, with strength renew'd, my bed;
From that defenceless state I live,
　　Which was the image of the dead.

Distant from me was every harm,
　　When I had been an easy prey;
But Lord, 'twas thine Almighty arm
　　Kept death and danger far away.

R

This day, may I securely pass,
    Protected by Almighty power;
Nor sin, or sorrow, find a place,
    Nor evil tidings meet my door.

Then be the guardian of my sleep,
    This day my all-sufficient guide,
And aid me right my heart to keep,
    Howe'er its tempted or is tried.

The joyful or afflicting scene,
    Goodness or wisdom shall prepare;
So may my thoughts by thee be seen,
    That blameless I may either share.

HYMN

SUNDAY EVENING.

———

AGAIN the shades of night advance,
  And close this blessed day,
For transient is earth's purest bliss,
  And sabbaths pass away.

A taste they give of future joys;
  But faint and transient here ;
Till we at Heaven's blest courts arrive,
  And find them purer there.

Oh ! may the truths this day has taught,
  Each Christian grace increase :
For Lord, we thank thee, this day's lot
  To us was health and peace.

No meaner pleasures from thy courts,
  Sure led our steps away ;

Nor in thy presence, earthly cares
   Could tempt our hearts to stray.

How did our praises and our prayers,
   Reviving zeal impart ;
And every theme that tun'd our tongues,
   With fervour warm the heart ?

How in the preacher's warning voice
   Did we his truths revere,
Receive them with an humble mind,
   Not with a critic ear ?

Nor sought we, in each sin condemn'd,
   To suit another's case ;
But in our own, with searching eye,
   Faithful each fault to trace.

Lord, if our service thro' the day,
   Was pleasing in thy sight,
We thank thy love for every grace,
   That kept our hearts aright.

To day those solemn vows were paid,
   Which should our souls refine ;
Lord may our service thro' the week,
   And all our hearts be thine.

A

SUNDAY EVENING's HYMN,

IN SICKNESS.

MY fainting heart my God would praise,
  And tune my trembling tongue ;
Review his love thro' all my days,
  And bid my faith be strong.

Tho' from his house his chast'ning hand,
  Withheld my languid frame ;
His altar in my heart shall stand,
  And there I'll bless his name.

I'll count his mercies as they rose,
  And thanks for each employ ;
For nights of peace and calm repose,
  And days of health and joy.

For friends, who form'd my mind with care,
   For all my means of grace ;
Shall impious doubts then check my prayer,
   Tho' now he veils his face ?

Resign'd, I wait a heavenly birth,
   When God shall call me home ;
Gently he weans my heart from earth,
   My father bids me come.

If earthly sabbaths are no more,
   I'll ask a seraph's lyre ;
My spirit would delighted soar,
   And join the heavenly choir.

EVENING HYMN.

HOW quick the passing hours have fled,
   And days how fast they speed;
And morning light, and evening shade,
   With rapid haste succeed.

Still now the busy hand of toil,
   Our sun lights other skies;
To him whose favors on me smile,
   My evening praises rise.

Of blessings which my life has brought,
   I'm lost in the survey;
For scarcely could I number out
   The mercies of this day.

The health, the peace, the social joy,
   My happy hours have shar'd;

For all my wants a rich supply,
   Was thro' this day prepar'd.

No irksome toil my time opprest,
   Or sloth supinely lost ;
With social ease, it still was blest,
   Or pleasing cares could boast.

I thank my God who led me on,
   His statutes to pursue,
For any good my hand has done,
   And all I wish'd to do.

And now I lay me down to rest,
   Beneath his guardian care :
Unless his wisdom think it best,
   No danger shall come near.

AN

EVENING HYMN,

IN SICKNESS.

———

MY strong support, my sov'reign king,
  Oh, deign to hear my evening vows;
Submission to thy will I bring,
  In humble trust my spirit bows.

Let ceaseless thanks my heart employ,
  For life, thy loving kindness gave;
And health, and powers to make it joy,
  And friends my heedless youth to save.

My life I fondly have review'd,
  Thy love in ev'ry stage to see;
And now for all departed good,
  My heavenly friend shall be to me.

Thro' all the sorrows I have felt,
  A parent's tender care appears;
To know they were in mercy dealt,
  Subdues my doubts, dispels my fears.

Now let my slumbering conscience wake,
  I'll bid my cherish'd sins depart;
Patient each bitter portion take,
  And let it purify my heart.

I'll humbly seek my father's love,
  There pardon dwells, there rich reward:
A contrite heart his mercies move,
  To be my safety and my guard.

In all my wants he's rich to give,
  In all my weakness strong to save;
His conquering son has bid me live,
  And brighten'd sickness and the grave.

END OF THE HYMNS.

LANCASTER CASTLE,

BY MOONLIGHT.

NOW the full moon departed day supplies,
　Her ray serene invites me here to stray :
Hail her in azure, queen of spangled skies ;
　And bless the chearer of the traveller's way.

But chief, beneath these venerable towers,
　I find the scenes for contemplation fraught ;
Congenial scenes to solitary hours,
　Congenial to the muse of pensive thought.

Within yon grates, now twinkling lights dispense
　Their little blaze, to those who durance 'bide ;
Along those battlements the moon beams glance,
　And o'er that awful portal shadows glide.

Thou ancient pile! whose founder sleeps unknown,
    But since to ages, first he gave his plan,
Full many a change has Britain's empire shewn,
    And pass'd has many a race of feeble man.

How far remote, tradition spares to say ;
    Nor found its date in legend's fertile page ;
But mould'ring time has wrought it no decay ;
    Nor has it felt the shock of hostile rage.

While low full many a noble fabric lies ;
    By savage fray, or time subdu'd at length ;
Genius still kind to thee its aid supplies*,
    Adds grandeur to thy grandeur, strength to
      strength.

Here station'd, to her gods their altars rose†,
    When Rome of Britain took her transient hold ;
This site, her skilful warriors early chose ;
    And seated here, annoy'd the foe so bold‡.

---

* The grand and useful improvements making by Mr. Harrison, will long bear an honourable testimony to his genius.

† An altar dedicated to Mars has been found in making the present improvements.

‡ The Caledonians.

When jarring nations and long time had pass'd,
   This front thy royal Gaunt thus bid arise;
Summon'd some H - - - n, in gothic taste,
   With solemn grandeur to attract all eyes.

Sublime thy fabric, and how fair around,
   Survey'd by day the lovely view appears!
But faded now, as tints in memory's found,
   When it would draw for age its youthful years.

Tho' distant hills are wrapp'd in clouds of night,
   And vivid colours mix in graver shade;
Where first I breath'd the air and saw the light,
   With rapture still, my native town's survey'd.

Oft from its streets my eye well pleas'd I cast,
   On verdant hills, whence rose its early name*;
And still, a little tribute to the past,
   It yet retains, in part, its ancient claim†.

Here oft in infancy with awe I've trod,
   Hearing of secret caverns deep and drear;
And many a winding subterranean road,
   Wond'ring why man his fellow man should fear

---

* The Saxon name was Green Town.

† That part of Lancaster called Green Acr.

Quitting the calm serene that sooths around,
    Within these walls humanity shall turn;
Think on the holds where human misery's found,
    And ask for whom those glimmering tapers burn.

Some there, perhaps, were rear'd with fondest pride,
    Wore rich attire, and fed on costly fare;
But now, of common liberty denied,
    And the free current of the vital air.

Ye fallen! where are now those crouded calls,
    That throng'd from dissipation's giddy train?
Say, need there massy bolts and lofty walls,
    To banish friends when fortune's on the wane?

But scenes more solemn still attend my way,
    As thro' the church-yard path I pensive tread;
Yon gloomy towers, alas! no light display,
    And all is silent as the sleeping dead.

Save where a shriek for mercy strikes the ear,*
    Which ah! if pity hear, it hears in vain;
For daring vice is stopp'd in mad career,
    And awful justice holds its rigid reign.

---

* The convicts under sentence of death.

O'er sanguinary laws the good must mourn,
   And breathe a wish, that nations, generous, great,
To other modes, for warning soon would turn,
   And death assign but for the murderer's fate.

Oh ye whose nights are ease, and days delight,
   Think on the prisoner in his lonely cell ;
Within whose heart, thro' all his long dark night,
   Bitter reflections, sad forebodings dwell.

Him, his fond mother nurs'd with tender love,
   Joy'd in his growth, guarded his health with care,
Thought not of hardship, when for him she strove,
   And for his good her little all would spare.

Alas! a tempting world seduced his youth,
   And from a virtuous course his heart could steal,
Maternal tears he scorn'd and warning truth,
   Which adds a pang to all he's doom'd to feel.

He thro' his days of bondage deeply mourns,
   Waters his little garden with his tears*,
In thought, to times of innocence returns,
   When simple pleasures charm'd his harmless years.

---

* The Crown Prisoners in Lancaster Castle have small gardens.

Ye good, with gentle counsels calm his heart !
    Increase his comforts, you, where much is given,
Spare tears from-fictions, pity here impart,
    From follies spare, to take your hold on Heaven !

H - - n, to thee my Muse glad tribute pays,
    Long ere thy gentle spirit is set free ;
Be painful duties soothed by general praise,
    And soft humanity dispensed by thee.

May all who bind the bonds the wretched bear,
    And hold dominion in their sad'abode ;
With lenient hand fulfil their task severe,
    And have their mercy shewn, to plead with God.

May thy pitying spirit here pervade,
    Howard, thy generous efforts still avail ;
The cell of bondage fewer woes invade,
    For man with man may mercy still prevail.

With Howard's name revered my song shall close,
    For him what trophies shall Britannia raise ?
In distant lands his ashes must repose,
    Her prisons be his monuments of praise.

THE END.